WALL OF FIRE

MELANIE TAYS

Published by Goldlight Enterprises LLC
Published in Queen Creek, Arizona, USA

Library of Congress Control Number: 2020902001

ISBN: 978-1-952141-01-0 (paperback)
ISBN: 978-1-952141-00-3 (ebook)

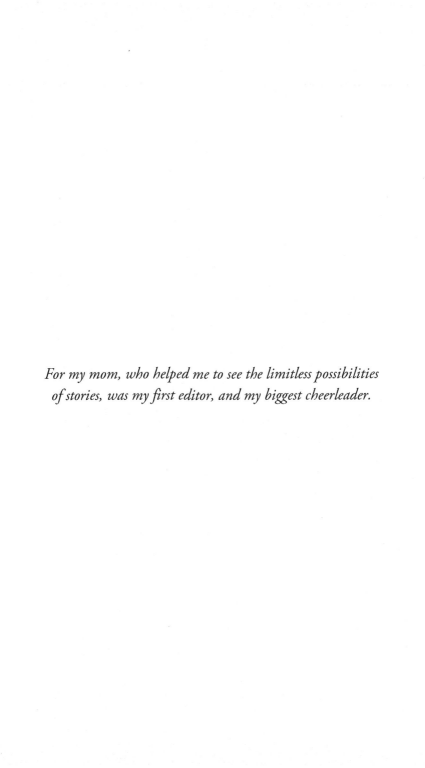

For my mom, who helped me to see the limitless possibilities of stories, was my first editor, and my biggest cheerleader.

CHAPTER 1

The sky is endlessly blue—just as it has been every day of my entire life—and it feels like a prison. It's supposed to make us all feel safe, but for some reason I can't quite grasp, it always feels wrong to me. Clouds, rainbows, and the sun—things I've only heard of in stories—seem to call to me from somewhere beyond. Of course, it's not really the sky at all, just a projection on the barrier field that encompasses The City in a protective dome, sparing us from sight of the horrors it holds at bay.

"Mina!" someone calls from behind, and a heavy hand claps down on my shoulder.

I sigh. As I turn, Liam does a quick double-take and then rips his hand away as if the mere sight of my face has burned him.

"Oh, it's you, E..." He runs his fingers awkwardly through his messy brown hair, letting my name trail off as he realizes that, despite the fact that we are only one year apart in school, he's not quite sure what my name actually is—Emmaline, Ember, Ebony...

"Emery," I mutter and turn away, hoping he'll just move on, but he doesn't take the hint. Apparently he was not specifically looking for Mina, and anyone to fill the silence with will do.

"It's just that when I saw Mina—or thought I saw Mina, because your long hair looks pretty similar from behind—I wanted to ask her how her dad was doing," he says. "He was really sick, you know."

"I didn't know." I try to infuse my tone with the added sentiment that he can go ahead and spare me the details.

Mina is several years younger than me. We know each other, but not well. Her dad being unwell isn't really news. Just last month, my own father had to have two fingers on his left hand reattached after a malfunction at the metal recycling plant severed them. Things happen. It's just life.

I start walking again and enter the queue for breakfast. Unfortunately, Liam follows and takes his place in line directly behind me.

"More people than usual have been coming into the Medical Center the last few weeks," Liam says, clearly hoping to capture my interest. He fails. You don't survive in the Smoke by getting involved in things that aren't your problem, and this sure isn't mine.

Refreshing silence hangs between us as people receive their trays of food and we press closer to the window. I search the nearby tables for my younger brother, Whyle, and find him two tables over, staring at his half-eaten tray. It's typical for him to rush through his meals, but that's just so he can play with the other kids before school starts. I'm surprised to see him still sitting there and not eating. Something must be wrong. I hope that snotty ten-year-old, Kline, didn't tell Whyle that he's too young to be on their team again. If he did, I'm going to have some choice words for him. Whyle may only be eight, but he's faster than any of the other kids.

I pick up a pebble from the ground and toss it to get Whyle's attention. My aim is perfect as always, and it lands squarely on the tray, not even touching the uneaten food, drawing the admiring gaze of a few people who happened to notice. He raises his head and turns to see who threw it. I wave and grin, but all I get in return is a weak upturn of one side of his mouth that can't even honestly be classified as a smile.

Whyle is about the most expressive and exuberant kid there is, so his reaction only heightens my sense of unease.

I've almost forgotten about Liam when his need to fill the silence with anything he can think of gets the better of him, and he says, "Are you going to join?"

"What?" I ask, distracted.

He gestures toward the faded sign hanging on the wall near the food dispensary window, reminding us all that today is the beginning of the next round of the Burning.

I laugh, but my eyes are drawn involuntarily to the Wall of Fire standing not far in the distance behind Liam. Flames lap from the ground up into the air, reaching twice my height. The blazing barricade separates the entire city center—the Flame—from the perimeter where we live—the Smoke.

There's only one way for us to cross the Wall of Fire,

and a limited window of time to do it. The Burning occurs twice each year. Anyone who is seventeen can join—giving each of us two opportunities to decide to go. Pass the gauntlet of tests and you earn a permanent place in the Flame. But if you try and fail the Burning, you will be expelled beyond the barrier field to the Ash to fend for yourself among the Roamers.

"If I wanted to be sent to the Ash, I could think of easier, less humiliating ways to go," I reply.

Liam opens his mouth to say something else, so I turn his question around on him to cut him off. "It's not like you went when you had the chance."

"Yeah, well..." he mutters.

There's really nothing to say, because we all know why he didn't go last year when he was seventeen, and why I won't go now. It's only once every year or two that someone from the Smoke actually joins. No matter how dismal life's prospects might be here—with long, grueling work days, buildings that collapse without warning, and the same gray mush for three meals a day—at least we can count on what we've got.

How could we ever hope to pass the Burning when we're competing against those who grew up in the Flame, trained by teachers and parents who have passed the Burning themselves?

Occasionally, someone gets the idea that they're going to train for the Burning, but I can't see what the point is when not a single person in the Smoke can tell you a solid thing about what to expect. Once you go to the Burning, succeed or fail, the one thing you can never do is return to the Smoke. It's clearly rigged against us, and unless you're looking for a way out of The City—and soon thereafter out of life—we all know to steer clear of the Burning.

Thankfully, the awkward and pointless conversation comes to a halt as I reach the front of the line. I scan my ID card and am issued a metal tray laden with mush. It's a slightly redder hue of gray today. Sometimes they change the exact formula to make sure our dietary needs are optimally met. My stomach grumbles in anticipation of being filled, and I head for the table where Whyle sits alone. Our parents both work the early shift today. Their assignments change every few months, just like everyone else's. Right now, Mom is at the power plant and Dad at the metal recycler.

As I approach, my earlier impression that something is wrong with Whyle returns, and I don't think it's just social angst. He's swaying in his seat and looking around in alarm. Before I reach him, Whyle collapses face down onto the table.

"Whyle!" I cry. I drop my tray into the dirt, not caring that I won't be allowed a replacement, and take off running for him.

Most people ignore the entire incident, but a few come over to check on the boy. He's young and here without his parents. Shoving past a woman who's trying to shake him awake, I take his head in my hands and raise it to look into his eyes. They are open slightly, but unfocused.

"Whyle! Whyle!" I shout into his face, but there's no

reaction.

More people start to gather, and I know most of them are wondering if the boy's food is going to be abandoned. I've lived here long enough that I don't have to look back to know that my food has already been scooped from the dirt and devoured behind me.

A man steps forward and reaches for Whyle. "I'll carry him to the Medical Center," he offers. I recognize him as one of the men that works with Dad, though I don't know his name.

"I've got him," I insist, hoisting Whyle over my shoulder with lumbering effort.

"Don't be silly," the man says. "Let me help."

"I've got him," I snap back, and the crowd parts to let us through.

Thankfully, the Medical Center is just across the street. Still, Whyle is heavier than the fifty-pound bags of dirt I sometimes haul for the repair crews, and I'm feeling the strain by the time I reach the entrance.

"Here, let me get the door for you," Liam says. I guess I didn't manage to shake him off after all.

"Thanks."

"This way." He starts to lead me to the left, away from the usual check-in desk.

When I begin to protest, he says, "I can get him right to a bed. I'm assigned to work here now."

So that explains both his knowledge of and interest in Mina's father's illness.

With back and legs burning under the weight I carry, I

follow him through a gray and dusty curtain and around a corner. This brings us to a long row of beds, each surrounded by a waist-high wall. The first two beds are occupied by one woman and one girl who can't be much older than six, both of them unconscious. Liam stops at the third bed and reaches for Whyle. I resist the urge to push him away; accepting a little help is better than accidentally dropping Whyle head-first on the concrete. A concussion isn't likely to be the antidote to whatever has seized his body and left him limp and moaning with eyes rolling behind half-open lids.

While I straighten my brother's legs on the bed, Liam races away. By the time I have Whyle tucked beneath a blanket, Liam has returned with two doctors in tow.

"Another one?"

The first doctor rushes to Whyle's side. Her brow is furrowed, and she looks like she hasn't slept in days.

Her companion sweeps a hand-held scanner over Whyle from head to toe. I would guess he's about my dad's age, and though his body is less worn down from manual labor, his eyes convey a different kind of strain he bears each day.

The two doctors ignore me and go to work on Whyle—placing a monitor on his forehead, inserting a needle into his arm, and injecting some kind of medication.

"What is that?" I demand. "What's wrong with him?"

The two doctors pay me no more attention than they would an insect buzzing overhead.

They can't ignore me like this. I need to know what's wrong with Whyle. More than that, I need to know that he's going to be okay.

"Hey, tell me what's wrong with my brother," I demand.

Sensing my distress, Liam pulls me away from the frenzied action. "Emery," he says, "let them work."

"What did they give him?"

"Just some medicine for the fever. They have to keep it down or it will cause brain damage."

I glance over and notice for the first time the beads of sweat rolling down Whyle's brow and neck. My own adrenaline was running so high when I carried him here that I didn't even realize how hot he felt. His shaggy black hair clings to his forehead. His face has settled into a disturbing shade of red, like blood is trying to burst through his flesh.

"Is it…?" I can't finish the question, but I don't have to. Liam knows what I must be asking—the first thing anyone would want to know.

"Not the Withers," he says.

His assurance should comfort me, because if the Withers has crept its deadly tentacles into The City—past the electromagnetic Safe Dome barrier erected twenty-two years ago to save us from its reach—then all hope for humanity really is lost. But Liam claims that it's not the Withers. Not the virus that made people appear as though their flesh was melting from their bones, that slowly disconnected people's bodies from the inside out. So why does Liam's face not give me hope as he says it? Has nature found a new horror to torture us with, like a dog taunting a rat before at last biting its throat?

"What, then?"

"We don't know." Liam gestures to the room at large. "Your brother is the fifth person to come in with the same symptoms in the last month."

I take in the sight of the other patients on the beds near Whyle. They are all unconscious, skin reddened. Occasionally, they jerk in random fits. But there are only three of them, if you include Whyle.

"Fifth? Then what happened to the other two? Are they better now?" I ask, hopeful.

"One person, Mina's father that I was telling you about earlier, was sick with the same symptoms. Now he's better. But that was a special case."

"What do you mean?"

"The doctors gave him Curosene—it's a medicine that was invented when they were trying to find a cure for the Withers. It kind of worked, too, just not fast enough to actually save anyone. But it really is kind of a miracle drug. It actually restores damaged DNA to its original form. One dose did the trick against this...whatever it is. The doctors don't know what's causing it, so they haven't named it yet."

I feel both hopeful and annoyed. "Okay, so let's give Whyle and everyone else a shot of Curosene, and we can all be on our way. What are you people doing here?"

The answer seems so simple and obvious that I can't

imagine why they haven't done it already. Is it a matter of credits to pay for the medication? That's definitely a possibility. Already I'm starting to strategize ways we can save up credits. For my birthday a few months ago, we started saving to buy me a new pair of shoes. I wiggle my toes and feel the holes. These will do for a little longer if Whyle needs the credits. If that's not enough, we can keep the lights off at home and skip meals—whatever it takes.

Liam frowns. "That was the last dose we had."

"You're telling me that the Flame can't make more?" I protest. "I thought they could make anything there with all the raw materials we keep stripping out of everything The City recycles. If we could make it once, we should be able to keep on making it forever."

He shakes his head. "The Council won't approve it."

"Making it, or sending it here?"

He raises his eyebrows and shrugs.

"What about the other person? You said five. Three are here, one got better. What happened to the other one?" I'm not sure I want to know the answer, but I need it.

Liam bites at his lower lip.

"Tell me," I whisper.

"He died two weeks after his first symptoms," Liam admits, pity seeping through his words.

I refuse to believe that's the only option, and that nothing can be done. Rather than stay here and listen to any more, I retreat to Whyle's side.

The doctors are slowing their efforts now, making notations on a tablet, covering him back up, preparing to leave.

"Is he going to be okay?" I demand.

The woman turns to me as though she's just noticed that I'm here. "We've done what we can for now."

"Will he die?"

The doctors exchange an uncomfortable glance. Probably most people are not so direct, but more than anything, I hate ambiguity. Whatever it is, just give it to me straight so I can deal with it.

It's the male doctor that speaks this time, his voice unsteady. "That's the way it's looking. No one has recovered so far, but we'll keep trying."

"Except for the man you gave Curosene to," I counter, seeking either confirmation or contradiction.

The doctor shoots Liam a chiding glance as he speaks. "Well yes, there was that. But that's not possible now. Nothing we have access to now seems to have any effect."

"Why won't the Council send more? Isn't there something you can say, something you can do?" I plead.

"There's no arguing with the Council. I'm sure they have a good reason," the woman says with a derisive smile. "I'm sorry." There's real empathy in her parting words.

"You better get to school," Liam says.

I don't move. The Enforcers won't enter the Medical Center to look for me. I'm safe here.

The two doctors and Liam leave me alone in the room

of unconscious suffering. I try to push everything and everyone out of my awareness until all I see is Whyle. He was fine just yesterday. Now he looks frail, his life fading.

I move his arm, making room for me to sit on the bed next to him because there's nowhere else to sit. I nestle his hand in mine and use the thin blanket to wipe the perspiration from his face.

I try to imagine what life will be like without this little beacon of joy to brighten the dreary nothing of each day. At the same time, I try desperately to suppress the understanding that life without Whyle is possible.

*   *   *

I lose track of time until the rumbling of my stomach brings me back to the present and I realize that several hours have passed. It's only now that I consider that other people should be here—my parents need to know about Whyle. But there's nothing Mom or Dad can do for Whyle right now other than fret over him, and I'm doing that enough for us all.

There has to be something that can be done, someone who can help. It's just one small vial of medication that we need. Surely there's a way to get it.

Old memories start to coalesce, and I inhale a sharp breath in excitement. I let go of Whyle's hand and slide off the bed. Away from his radiating warmth, the air feels cold; a shiver runs through me despite the perfectly regulated air temperature.

I should go straight to the power plant and tell Mom what happened. I should go to school before the Enforcers catch me and dock me a day's worth of credits. Neither of those things will help Whyle now. But I just might know what—or rather, who—can.

CHAPTER 2

I keep to the back alleys as I make my way around the perimeter of The City. By doing this, I can avoid the Enforcers who usually just patrol the main square and the buildings that the Council considers of vital importance to the welfare of The City, such as the nutrition stations and the seven recycling centers that reclaim everything from plastics to human debris.

Nothing is ever wasted in The City.

I round a corner, and the makeshift building comes into view. From the outside it looks more like a pile of rubble, but it's probably one of the more structurally sound buildings in the Smoke, carefully constructed of bricks and boards that had come loose from other buildings and reinforced to make this shelter.

When I'm close, that's when I start looking for a fat, furry rat.

Rats are one of the few animals we have left in The City. Most of the birds, dogs, and pigs were illegally killed by people who just weren't satisfied with the food The City provides. I've only seen three birds in my whole life. Others—like turtles—died out on their own. People say something about the habitat not being right for them to thrive. The rats weren't even supposed to be a part of The City, but something went wrong with the original barrier field and let them in. Since rats can give birth to up to twelve live baby-vermin every single month, once they were inside, it proved impossible to eradicate them.

Still, they have their uses.

Whyle and I sometimes hunt them for fun, and I'm better at catching them than he is. They aren't smart. The key is just to approach quietly and pounce fast. The Council actually encourages it, because the rats are a threat—they eat some of the bugs and plants that we need to maintain our delicate ecosystem. It only takes me a few minutes to locate one of the scraggly, pointy-nosed pests, and less time to have it grasped firmly around the middle where it can't squirm free or twist around to bite me. Its fur is coarse and matted with dirt, which helps me keep a pretty solid grip, but I know the muscles in my hand will be aching with fatigue soon, so I need to get on with this.

With the rat hissing and writhing for its life and freedom, I approach the rubble pile that I know hides the safe house. It was several years ago when I stumbled into it. I came through here looking for a place to escape an Enforcer after he accused me of throwing a rock at his car. It wasn't true; he was just bored and in a foul mood, and somehow I got trapped in the fallout. My arms were completely full of heavy sacks loaded with recycled fabric at the time that I'd supposedly vandalized the vehicle. But the Enforcer didn't look like he was in a mood to be reasonable, so rather than wait around and try to explain that it couldn't have been me, I dropped the sacks and ran. I run fast, but I couldn't run forever, and he had a car.

Exhausted and unsure where to go, I crouched down next to the brick pile that forms one corner of the building. Through a small slit, I noticed two eyes staring out at me.

"In here," a woman whispered, and she pulled back a board to reveal an entrance.

I could hear the Enforcer's footsteps closing in, so I didn't think or argue; I just dove through the opening. That's how I met Kenna.

She's the one who opens the door now when I give the specific knock that calls for her. She hobbles out, hopping on just her right leg because her left leg was lost in an accident at the textile recycling center. When people can't work, they can't earn credits. That means no food, no shelter, nothing that The City provides. She holds a cane, but mostly just uses it to push things around. I never actually see it touch the ground.

Kenna is one of the lucky few who helped build this safe house, and has learned to survive on trades alone. If there's anything in the Smoke that can be gotten, she knows how to get it. But after that first meeting, I learned to never come asking for a favor empty-handed. We've had only a few interactions since that time, but she hasn't let me down yet.

"Whatcha got there?" she asks, hungrily eyeing the squirming rat.

"A big fat one." I hold it out to her.

She licks her lips. "Nice and fresh, too."

Most people don't eat the rats because they make you puke up your guts as often as not, but it's nothing you don't recover from. People in Kenna's situation have built up a tolerance, or so she's told me. I know that nothing will go to waste. The fur will add to a meager blanket, the bones might become toothpicks or sewing needles, or any number of other things that only someone so desperate would ever conceive of.

Now that she's seen that the rat hasn't been dead for days, I go ahead and bang its head hard against a brick. It's quick and effective, and its body instantly falls limp.

Kenna holds out her hands excitedly, but I pull it away.

"First, I need to know how to get some medicine."

She looks at me like I'm pretty stupid. "You don't want to get anything through my channels that you could get with credits. It'll be far more expensive. Just go to the Medical Center and they'll fix you right up."

"The Medical Center can't get it, either. I need Curosene, and the Council won't send more for some reason."

She whistles and shakes her head. "Oh sweetie, that kind of fancy medicine doesn't come through the back channels."

"There has to be some way to get it."

"If the Council has said it won't send more, there's no way to get it across the Wall of Fire."

I can't give up that easy. "Who else might be able to help me?"

"If I can't get you something, it can't be gotten this side of the wall," she insists. I know I've insulted her by suggesting that I might take my business to someone more capable. "Who got you those textbooks?" she says, reminding me of our last trade.

"You did," I admit.

Any books that aren't authorized by the Council for our school or work are forbidden. They say it's because unnecessary books make people so unhappy, but I've never been more content than when I've been able to fill in the gaping holes that my schooling leaves in understanding the world. Two thick books—one about math and science, and the other full of the history from before the Withers—cost me my extra shirt and pants and my breakfast for a whole month. These kinds of trades are never cheap—they're a desperate last resort.

I know she isn't exaggerating her ability. I've seen Kenna come through for people with seemingly impossible trades—power cells, ID cards, even an Enforcer's blaster. She is my only hope. That's why I can't walk away so easily.

"I'll pay anything," I promise. "My parents will, too. Kenna, you can have my house, for all I care. I just have to have that medicine." My voice breaks. Moisture gathers at the corners of my eyes, and I blink it away.

That gets her attention away from the dead critter I'm still clutching. She observes me for a moment, considering. "Well, for a house, maybe there's something I can do—but there's no going back on a trade," she warns me.

My offer was desperate and impulsive, but still I breathe a sigh of relief. "I swear. If you come through with that medicine, you can have my house." I can't stop to consider what that will mean for my family, but if Whyle dies, what does anything matter, anyway?

She twists her mouth and cocks her head to the side. "I've got a guy who deals in drugs. How about I get you a double dose of Amphetomite? That'll make any problem feel like it's nothing at all."

I groan. "Yeah, 'cuz you'll be so brain numb."

"Or I could get you a whole bottle of antivirals—kills anything weaker than the Withers."

"Kenna, you're not listening! I need Curosene. Nothing else."

"No, you're not listening, girl." She raps her cane lightly against my skull. "You clearly don't get how these things work. In order for my people to get something, it has to be here, in the Smoke, somewhere for us to get our hands on. That means that it either has to be produced here, the Council has to authorize it to be sent across the wall, or people like the Enforcers or couriers who come from the Flame each day have to carry it with them. You said the Council won't send this medicine, and why would anyone be just walking around with it in their pocket? They won't—so it ain't going to happen." She doesn't appear one bit happy to have to tell me this. The prospect of a proper house had already started to settle in and plant seeds of hope that would hurt to root out now.

"Is there any way to get across the wall? Surely someone has done it?" I ask. "The Enforcers and couriers go back and forth every day, so there must be a way."

She lets out a high-pitched whistle. "You are looking for trouble in every direction, ain't you? You have to have one of their fancy black armbands to get through the gates. It's their ID. Without it, forget it. You'll be arrested for even trying."

I can't accept that. "What about the tunnels?" I ask in desperation.

She laughs. "There ain't no tunnels, girl. Just a myth, a trap to see who's dumb enough to go looking." She holds out her hand for the rat, signaling that she has nothing more to say.

I grudgingly hand it over and walk away, feeling further away from a solution than ever. I can see the glow of the Wall of Fire in the distance. Whyle's salvation lies just on the other side, but it might as well be on the other side of the planet—past the barrier field and the Ash and the hordes of Roamers.

I'm not as careful as I head back toward the Medical Center. There are no Enforcers to avoid because its lunchtime and school is out for the day. In the afternoon, we all have our own work assignments. The Enforcers take work assignments a lot more seriously than school, so I'll have to show up and assist the building repair crew where I'm currently assigned, whether or not I like it.

A rumbling ache builds from deep inside, but I put off lunch for just long enough to go find Mom. She won't forgive me if she has to find out about Whyle from a stranger, and I suppose I can't blame her.

CHAPTER 3

Mom sits next to Whyle, bent over him as though she's attempting to shelter him from some external danger. But it's what's inside him that's the real threat. Her tears have run dry, but they've washed uneven lines from the soot covering her face. Dad stands solemnly behind her with a hand on her shoulder in solidarity.

I can almost hear Whyle's gentle voice asking me if I'm all right. But of course, it's just in my imagination—an echo of the past. Whyle is always the first—and often only—person to notice when I'm troubled. From the time he was a baby, he's been looking out for me every bit as much as I've looked out for him. Even though it was rare he could do more for me than offer the feeble reassurances of a small child and give me flowers fashioned out of dried dirt, he always tried. That was usually enough to keep me going. But what now?

It's almost curfew, and we'll have to head home soon. The thought of spending the night with Whyle's bed empty in the next room feels so hollow. I'm holding myself together, though. I won't cry and give my parents one more thing to worry about.

Then Dad leans down next to Whyle and starts to talk about Oran, and I have to walk away because I just can't take it anymore. Oran is a dragon in the latest bedtime story that Dad is telling Whyle. Each night more of the saga unfolds, revealing Oran's adventures and how he transforms from bad to good. It turns out that he was never evil, just confused. Whyle never sleeps well if Dad isn't there to tell a story. Mom and I have both tried to fill in for him on nights he's had to work late, but neither of us seems to have the knack for storytelling that Dad does. Even though Whyle is unconscious, I guess Dad wants to give Whyle whatever small bit of peace he can offer.

I pace up and down the aisle. Mom told me when I was little that I paced like a pendulum when I got nervous, and that I should put my energy to better use, so I rarely pace anymore. But the need to act is like an electric charge coursing through my veins and gnawing at me from the inside. The problem is that there's nothing to be done right now that's of any use whatsoever. The only thing that can help Whyle now is across the Wall of Fire—inexorably out of reach. The pain of it is visceral, and eased only the slightest degree by the rhythmic motion of my feet.

There has to be something I can do to help Whyle—to hear him beg for one more story and laugh at the most fantastic and silliest things Dad comes up with. But I do believe Kenna—there's no way to get that medicine in the Smoke, and reaching the Flame is impossible.

The rumbling of an engine—something fairly rare—draws my gaze to the window. Welcoming a distraction, I take a few steps closer to get a better view of what's happening outside. I peer out into the dimly lit street where a courier truck has stopped, and a man hauling a heavy crate ambles slowly across the road in front of it. Halfway across, he drops the crate and bends to gather what look like nails. Until the mess is cleared, there's no way for the vehicle to proceed without destroying its tires.

While the vehicle idles, a man with a cane hobbles up to the Enforcer who accompanies this transport—every courier travels with a guard. I can't hear what he's saying, but it looks like he's asking a series of questions. The Enforcer responds with annoyance.

I cautiously slide the window open to listen, but I still can't make out their words.

While the Enforcer is talking and distracted, another man wearing a sweater with a hood that shades his face creeps around to the backside of the vehicle and steps up on a high ledge. He's careful to not make a sound, so it takes him a minute of careful manipulation to work open the window at the top and reach inside. I watch, stunned by the brazen action, as he removes a large, heavy sack from the truck's cargo. He heaves it over his shoulder, steps carefully down, and starts casually walking.

Just then the road clears, and the man with the cane thanks the Enforcer for his time and starts to walk off. All three of them head in different directions as though they're completely unconnected, but I'm certain that the entire scene was a coordinated effort.

The truck rolls on, and I begin to think they've gotten away with their carefully constructed theft when the truck comes to a screeching halt and the courier jumps out and points in the direction of the thief, not yet out of sight.

Spotted, the thief takes off running, and the Enforcer jumps from his perch on a ledge along the truck's passenger side. "Don't wait. Get across the wall," the Enforcer yells to the driver, loud enough that I can make out the words from where I stand.

The driver hesitates for just a moment, unsure what to do. He's not supposed to travel without an Enforcer, but staying here stationary and unguarded is a bigger danger, and would also mean disobeying a direct order.

The Enforcer takes off running after the perpetrator.

The driver may be hesitating, but I'm not. Perhaps I'm emboldened by such a reckless and daring act, or perhaps I'm just desperate. Either way, the moment the Enforcer turns his back, I realize that this may be the only chance I'll ever have to get across the Wall of Fire. There's no time for deliberation. I bound out of the open window. The driver is facing away from me, so I break into an open run for the vehicle.

By the time I reach its side, the driver has started to move again. All I can do is jump onto the ledge where the Enforcer would normally stand. My foot catches the step, and my right hand grasps the handhold. The vehicle is moving slowly, so it isn't too difficult to steady myself. I crouch down and press myself as close as I can to the metal wall of the truck.

Thankfully, the streets are mostly deserted since it's close to curfew. Mom and Dad will be heading home any minute, and I wonder what they'll make of my absence. I know they won't be too worried, though; they always trust me to look out for myself. It would be Whyle who would be concerned about me, and Whyle who would make them go looking for me. But Whyle won't even know I'm gone tonight.

Still, I can't very well stay here, exposed. The truck is picking up speed, and I have to get inside before we reach the Wall of Fire. The entrance to the cargo area is ten feet back. A bar runs along the top, but the side is sheer, smooth metal with nowhere at all to get a foothold. I can see a ledge at the back of the truck, a place for me to put my feet and launch myself in through the back window. I just have to get there first.

Before I even make a move, sweat is already moistening my palms. I wipe them on the legs of my pants and take a deep breath to steel my nerves. Then, before I have too long to think about what I'm going to do, I jump for the bar, clasping it with both hands. Slowly, I inch my way back, my feet dangling several feet above the rapidly passing, dusty street.

I'm only a few arm's lengths away from my destination when the wheels hit a large dip in the road, and the vehicle sways. My left hand loses its grip completely, and I swing awkwardly by one arm, crashing into the metal side with a thud.

I don't have time to worry whether the driver heard the clatter and will stop to investigate. My fingers are slick and slipping. I swing and reach for the bar, but my hand is too damp with sweat to get a hold. I press my left palm against the side of the vehicle, trying desperately to find purchase. There's nothing to grasp, of course, but the dust that coats the metal has the unexpected benefit of drying the moisture from my palm. I swing again and reach, and this time my hand grasps the bar just as my right hand slips free. I rub it against the dirty siding as well, and then continue working my way along the bar, hands and arms protesting in pain.

The driver doesn't slow, so he either didn't hear the clatter I made or assumed it was merely shifting cargo. Either way, I'm grateful.

With a sigh of relief, I reach the ledge at the back. The window is still propped open slightly from the theft, and I quickly scurry into the cargo hold. It's full of sacks that I recognize from the nutrition stations. When the contents of these bags are mixed with the right amount of water, you get the gray mush that makes up our diet. I'm not sure why they're taking this back with them into the Flame, but I also don't care. I consider moving all the way to the back of the piled sacks, but it's a balance between not being discovered and being able to make a quick escape at the first opportunity. Carefully, I shift a few of the bags and manage to nestle down out of sight behind the second row.

The wave of adrenaline that pulled me out of the

window and into this truck begins to subside, but a new wave hits—this one brought on by the realization of what I've just done. Suddenly, I'm panicking, wondering if it's too late to leap from the truck and abandon this reckless plan that's almost certainly doomed to failure.

But as soon as I think of climbing from my hiding place and escaping back into the safety of the Smoke, the truck begins to decelerate and I see the glow of the Wall of Fire dancing through the window above. I've lost my chance to turn back. My only hope now is to go forward—to get across unseen, find the medicine, and return.

CHAPTER 4

Soon we lurch to a full stop, and the driver greets someone.

"Where's Garrick?" the guard at the wall asks the driver.

"We were robbed in the streets. He went after them with instructions for me to come straight here, no stops."

"Blazes, the Resistance is such a nuisance," the man says. "I can't imagine what they think they're going to accomplish. If they want to go to the Ash, we should just have a release form. Anyone who wants out can just sign it and go to their death for all I care."

"The Council is too kind for that. Those people don't have any idea what they're really talking about."

I've never heard of a Resistance, or anyone *wanting* to go to the Ash. Those guys were probably just hungry and looking for a few extra meals. Or maybe they'll trade it to someone like Kenna for light bulbs, or shoelaces, or something else as innocuous and hard to come by as that.

"Has it started?" the driver asks.

"In about ten minutes," the man responds. "I'll get you through quickly and you can still make it."

I don't know or care what they're talking about; I just

like the part about getting through here quickly. That probably means no inspections.

"Thanks. My son is going," the driver explains.

"Oh, Ty will do great, I'm sure. Bright kid," the guard assures him.

"Thanks. I think so, too. As a parent, though, it's difficult to not be a little nervous."

The guard makes one last comment about his own kids, and then the truck begins to roll again. I can't help noticing how smooth the ride is on this side of the wall; no pebbles and cracks for the wheels to contend with. The driver pulls the truck under a canopy and shuts off the engine. I hear him open his door, climb down, and slam it shut. He yells a final goodbye to the man who let us through the gate, and his footsteps fade away.

Cautiously, I wriggle my way free of my hiding place and approach the window at the back of the vehicle. I can see the man that we just passed. He's standing near an archway in the Wall of Fire. He does something on a control panel next to him, and the archway collapses into flames, sealing the conduit between the sectors. With his post secured, he walks away in the same direction that the driver just headed.

I pause and listen, but hear nothing except some shouts and cheers in the distance. It feels too good to be true, but I'm almost positive that I've just been left here alone. I remind myself that it's not like they know I'm here, so why wouldn't they leave? I can't count on any degree of luck holding, so I can't waste this. I climb out, ready to go.

I know nearly nothing about The City on this side of the wall, so from this point on, I'll have to make up the plan as I go—not that I had a well-thought-out plan before. I take a moment to look around and get my bearings. The Wall of Fire burns like a beacon behind me, assuring me that this is still The City, but everything feels different—too perfect, too clean, too well held together. Even the air tastes wrong somehow.

There are a dozen other courier vehicles parked in a row. I take a few minutes, peeking into each. Some of them have supplies brought from the Smoke, just like the vehicle I came in. I assume they'll all be unloaded in the morning. Two of them are completely empty. It isn't until the second-to-last one that I find what I was hoping for: it's full of waste receptacles. There's no doubt that this is headed to the Smoke in the morning, to be delivered to the various recycle centers. Once I get the medicine, I'll make my way back here and hide out inside. There's no reason for them to check the cargo carefully in the morning. Who would ever want to sneak *out* of the Flame? I'll just wait until the driver unwittingly transports me home.

I wish I had a map of the Flame, but they don't exist back home because why would we ever need such a map? I'll have to search until I find the Medical Center. I start to move back the way I just came, between the vehicles and the swaying flames of the wall. As I slowly creep along, I let my fingers reach out and touch the Wall of

Fire. The flames lap at my hand and tickle. Of course, it's not real fire. If it were, the air recycling system could never keep up with The City's oxygen demands, with miles of fire wall continually gobbling it up. No, the wall is just a synthetic fire and an impenetrable barrier field, much like the dome that encapsulates The City.

"Is someone there?" a man shouts, ripping me from my stupid and reckless reverie.

I drop to the ground and roll under the nearest truck, fighting to keep my anxious breathing quiet and steady. I never should have let myself get distracted. There's too much at stake. Footsteps are coming closer, and then they pause just a few feet away. Carefully, I slide on my belly, pulling myself forward across the smooth pavement by my elbows in a clumsy crawl.

I make it to the next truck's underside, tucking my feet out of sight just as the man bends down and peers into the space I occupied moments ago. I freeze and wait, terrified that if I move again, I'll draw his attention for sure. All he has to do is turn his head slightly to the side and I'll be caught.

But his head doesn't turn. He straightens, and soon his footsteps resume in a calm and rhythmic pattern. He must have decided he was just seeing shadows and that there was nothing to worry about after all.

I sigh in relief and wait as he meanders around for a few more minutes before completing whatever business brought him here and departing. Several more minutes pass before enough of my fear and tension dissipate that I can finally make my muscles work again. I crawl out from under the truck, but stay low as I keep moving.

When I reach the end of the last truck, I peer cautiously down the street, careful to stay in the shadows. A few people are out walking, but they all appear to be heading toward the city center where an enormous torch burns, visible all the way from here. That's the direction all the noise is coming from, as though most of the Flame is gathering there for some reason. I can only assume that the Flame must not have the same curfew we do. Whatever the cause, it appears to be clearing the streets and working in my favor.

A torch burns at every street corner, casting far too much light for safety. I press my back against the wall and take tentative steps. The ground feels wrong beneath my feet—too smooth and slick, not a single broken brick or speck of dirt in sight. When I reach the end of the building, I cautiously peer around the corner. It leads to an empty alley that's dark from end to end. I turn the corner and run full out until I reach the other side.

"Hurry," a man calls.

I duck back into the shadows and freeze as a man and two small children run past, clearly not wanting to be late for whatever is about to transpire.

I breathe a sigh of relief and keep moving.

I pass through several alleys that separate houses, but this is clearly the wrong area. The Medical Center won't be located with the residences. It will be with the other service buildings, which I fear is right where all the people are now congregating. I might need to find a place to hide and wait until the commotion dies down.

"Stop!" a voice exclaims behind me.

I freeze and turn slowly, just in time to see a woman stick her head out a window and call to a boy about Whyle's age down on the street.

"Get back in here. This has nothing to do with us. You're going to bed."

The boy whines a little and walks with shuffling, heavy steps back to the door. He pauses when he spots me, and I hold my breath as though that might make me less noticeable.

"Get in this house right now," the woman bellows even louder, all patience exhausted.

The boy sticks his tongue out at me and races up the steps to the front door, disappearing inside. The woman closes the window with a thud, and I'm momentarily struck by how perfect the glass is—no cracks or dirt. I don't dwell on it long, though. Now that the coast is clear, I turn and run, not waiting to see if the boy will mention the strange, ragged girl lurking in the street.

I don't stop running until I've made several turns and am well out of sight and reach if the boy reports me to his mother and she calls the Enforcers. Once I'm sure that I won't be found easily, I stop to get my bearings and decide where to go next.

I realize with trepidation that in my haste to escape, I fled right to the edge of the city center, where hundreds of people are now gathered in the open plaza.

Onlookers cheer from the periphery, surrounding a group of teenagers who are all dressed in clothing more beautiful than I have ever laid eyes on, with hair styled and faces painted. I press my back against the wall of the nearest building and wait, but no one is looking my way.

Cautiously, I peek out. It doesn't take long to realize that all the important buildings are located in a circle, facing the torch at the center. Almost directly across from where I now crouch in the darkness lies a large white building with a sign above the entrance which confirms that this is the Medical Center. I'm so close.

I imagine myself back home, clasping Whyle's hand while the doctors administer the medicine that will restore him to perfect health, leaving no trace or suspicion that Emery Kennish ever crossed the Wall of Fire.

The only problem is that there's no way I can see to reach the Medical Center without stepping out into the open. I retreat into seclusion to consider my options.

I could try to make my way around the outer rim of the circle, hiding between buildings, and hope to avoid being seen. But there are so many people. It doesn't seem like a wise plan. Whatever this gathering is can't go on all night. I decide that my best option is to hunker down and hide until the streets clear. I have hours before that vehicle will leave for morning deliveries. There's no need to take unnecessary risks.

I retreat farther into the darkness between the buildings. Around me, a few waste receptacles have been left out for the recyclers to pick up. Other than that, the entire area has been swept clean, and there's nothing to offer any shelter. I crawl behind the receptacles and wrap my arms around my knees, pulling them tight to my chest, preparing for a long wait.

But it isn't long before the sounds of the crowd shift. I can't see what's happening, but people are moving now. I don't dare attempt a glance. I just stay hidden and pray that no one comes this way. But my fears are unnecessary; the crowd begins a procession through the streets, away from where I hide.

Within minutes, the noise is distant and muffled. I crawl out and tiptoe to the end of the building to look. The plaza that was packed with people just minutes before is now completely deserted.

It seems too good to be true, but I don't hesitate. I dart out and run hard and fast toward the Medical Center. I slam into the outer wall of the building to arrest my momentum. A move like that could do serious structural damage to a building in the Smoke, but the wall holds fast here.

I crouch down and stay near the wall as I move around to the side, relieved as the shadows swallow me once again. At the first window I come to, I risk a glance inside to reveal a fully lit patient ward with at least three doctors walking around, tending to the sick.

I drop back down before anyone notices me, and I amble, hunched to stay below the window line, until I reach the back of the building.

I round the corner, and my heart leaps at the sight

awaiting me. Stacked near the back door, waiting to be brought in, is a delivery of supplies. I don't even have to hope or guess at what's inside—they're all labeled. They contain bandages and a dozen different medicines, but none of that matters to me. Tears of relief well up in my eyes as they land on the only word that holds any meaning for me in this moment. *Curosene* is clearly written on the third box down.

Focused on my goal, I take one enthusiastic step forward.

"Stop right there and turn around," an authoritative voice calls out from behind.

CHAPTER 5

It takes every ounce of willpower I have not to dart forward and grab for the box of medicine, not to try and make a desperate escape. But when I slowly turn, the blaster pointed at my chest confirms that an escape attempt would be counterproductive, to say the least.

"What are you doing here?" the Enforcer demands.

"I… I got lost," I stammer weakly, not sure how that's supposed to explain anything, but it's the only explanation I can think of that doesn't actually admit to anything.

He shines a light in my direction to get a better look at me. As he appraises my worn clothing and generally un-Flame-like appearance, his eyes squint as though something doesn't add up. Then his gaze lingers on my right wrist, which is suspiciously naked—no Flame ID band.

There's nothing I can say to help the situation. All I can do is stand still like a statue and wait to discover my fate while my heart pummels the inside of my chest like a fist trying to break through. He approaches and pats my pockets, looking for something. Fortunately, they're empty—except for my ID card, which he removes and examines.

Suddenly, his eyes widen, and he lets out a heavy sigh. "Blazes," he mutters, and he doesn't look one bit happy. He lowers the blaster and comes toward me, grabbing me roughly by the arm. "I swear, only a Smoker could get lost. We made it so simple. Come on." He leads me on foot down the street in the direction the procession traveled moments ago.

I'm more than a little confused. Where does he think I was going when I got lost? I search my mind for what possible rationale he could have come up with to explain my presence here tonight, but come up blank. I can only devote a corner of my attention to puzzling it out. My thoughts are still pulled back behind us to the Medical Center. The medicine calls to me from just yards away, beckoning me, taunting me. But there's nothing I can do about it now, as each step takes us father away. At least there's no doubt now that the medicine is here. I just have to find another opportunity to get at it.

We travel a few blocks through empty streets, and then we reach the crowd's new gathering place. They have congregated near the Wall of Fire around a three-story building surrounded by a menacing razor-wire fence. My heart sinks, but only a little. I'm not really surprised that the Enforcer is leading me to the Justice Building to await some kind of trial for crossing illegally. I can't say I'm looking forward to whatever punishment will be doled out. I haven't committed the unforgivable crime of murder, so I'll ultimately be sent home after punishment.

I just hope they decide quickly and administer the lashes, or whatever it'll be, before Whyle's time runs out.

I console myself with the thought that, now that I know how to get across the wall and where I need to go, I'll be smarter next time.

What doesn't make sense is the presence of everyone else. Why would they all have gathered here tonight as though it's some kind of special event?

The Enforcer pushes our way through the onlookers, who readily step aside for him. A guard stands at the gate up ahead; he has just admitted a girl about my own age. He calls something aloud, but it's muffled by the din of the onlookers, and I can't make out what he says.

A confused and surprised exclamation ripples through the masses as I'm brought to the gate. My tattered and filthy clothing alone make it clear that I'm from the wrong side of the wall.

The spool of my nerves winds tighter with every step. Whatever awaits me inside will be meant to teach me to never repeat my offense, and probably to deter others as well. I know that I can endure pain, though, if I have to. It's something else, beyond the anticipated pain, that has my insides vying for an opportunity to come out. I can't put a finger on what, but something just feels so wrong about this situation.

The Enforcer holds out my ID card that he removed from me earlier and hands it to the guard. The sneering guard holds the card by one corner, as though being from the Smoke is contagious. He scans the card, and the gate opens.

My captor pushes me through. It's not until I've passed the razor-wire fence that the golden archway in the nearby Wall of Fire comes into view, and I scream in terror.

"No!" I turn and lunge for the gate that has snapped shut behind me. The only place to take hold is cutting wire, but I don't care. I clasp the gate and rattle it as hard as I can, trying to shove my way back through and shredding my skin in the process.

"This is a mistake. I'm not supposed to be here," I plead.

My escort brings his blaster up and points it at my chest.

Over my screams and protests, the guard announces to the crowd, "Emery Kennish, contestant number twenty-seven of the Burning."

And then I hear the high-pitched shrill of the Enforcer's blaster firing straight at my chest.

*   *   *

I wake with a start and see flames beside me. I roll away and fall several feet with a thud.

"Oh, dear!" a woman exclaims in a wispy chime.

I pull myself up. In my stupefied state, what I thought was fire is actually just this tall, slender woman dressed in yellow and red sparkles from neck to ankles. Her hair is styled up in yellow spikes, all done to create the appearance that she is fire personified.

She frowns at me. "Not a good start, Emery. I'm quite disappointed."

"Huh?" I mutter, confused. I feel my chest and move all my muscles, assessing myself for damage. "Am I okay?"

"Of course. A stun blast will only knock you out for a little while," the woman explains as though speaking to a small child.

I examine my hands to see how badly I've injured them on the razor-wire fence, and am confused to find no trace of the injury except light pink lines crisscrossing my palms.

"The doctor fixed those right up for you," the woman says. "Don't fret about it. In an hour or so those ugly lines will be gone, too. I just hope you've learned your lesson about the fence."

The room is softly lit, light flowing from an overhead chandelier. I'm in an immaculate room next to a single bed, off of which I just tumbled to the sparkling tile floor. There's a window behind the woman. The sky outside is still dark, and it sounds like the crowd has not fully dissipated yet, though the clatter is unorganized and beginning to wane.

"I am Keya. I'll be your Burn Master," the woman goes on. "I will be guiding you through this exciting journey of discovery and purification to find the place in our society where you truly belong." She makes this wretched ordeal sound like some kind of spiritual journey of enlightenment.

I pull myself up off the floor. "Keya, listen, I didn't actually want to join the Burning. I just want to go home. Isn't there any way that you can help me get out of here? This was all just a big mistake."

She smiles knowingly. "I'm sure that this is all very overwhelming and disorienting for you," she says in a consoling tone. "You're not the first person to have second thoughts and trepidations after becoming a contestant. Most people wait until they're a trial or two into the process before having such a complete meltdown. However, what you're experiencing is totally normal, and you need to trust your first instinct that led you here. It shows that you have a desire within you to be something of true value to The City and humanity. Now it is your time to see if that's possible."

"But Keya, please, isn't there any way I can quit and just go home?"

"No, my dear," she says, the corners of her eyes turned down in sympathy.

I start to protest, to make one last plea, but she holds up her hand for silence.

"Emery," she says. "I know that things are different here than you're used to. But things are never going to be the same again. The sooner you accept that, the better your chances will be of surviving the Burning and receiving an assignment. That's what you have to focus on now, because your only other alternative—from the moment that you crossed the Wall of Fire—is the Ash." Her words are cold and direct, but something tells me that she's really trying to help me, and maybe even hopes that I'll pass the Burning.

I nod. There's really nothing else to say.

A knock sounds at the door, and Keya calls out, "Come in, come in," in a sing-song cadence, as though we've just been having a lovely, light-hearted chat this whole time.

A man in a dark suit enters clutching a small black case as though it holds something precious.

"There you are, Ronaldy," Keya greets him. "Perfect timing."

"Why don't you sit on the bed for this?" he suggests as he approaches me.

"For what?"

"Just sit," Keya says. "Remember, don't be difficult. This is all for your own good."

I strongly doubt that, but I take a seat anyway.

The man sets the case down on the bed next to me. Both Keya and Ronaldy hold their black wristbands next to a sensor, and the case's latch pops open. Inside rests an identical black band, just like the ones that everyone in the street was wearing.

I guard my arms. "What is that?"

"Why, it's your intercuff," she proclaims with pride, as though she's offering me a gift. "It's your identification. No more need to carry around a silly card. It will also give you messages about what you need to do, and can allow you to communicate with people. Not that you have anyone here to communicate with, but details, details…"

She waves her hand in the air like she's erasing something. "We all wear them here in the Flame. This is the first step to making you one of us."

I fail to show the proper enthusiasm, and her smile fades to a scowl.

"Okay, just put it on the nightstand and I'll be sure to wear it tomorrow," I say. "I'm very tired now. I should really get some rest."

"That's not how this works," the man states, his voice low and monotone. "Hold out your arm."

I would honestly prefer to cut off my own arm rather than let them affix that thing to me, but I'm not really given an option. Besides, based on how efficiently they healed my hands, I'm betting that if I tried this, they'd just sew me back up with the band already attached to my reconnected limb.

Without any real alternative, I hold out my right arm. The man clamps the band down around my wrist. I consider whether it's too tight to slip out of, but then he inserts a silver, notched pin into a small hole on the side. The sensation of a thousand needles jabbing my wrist assaults my nerves. I yelp, and then the pain is gone.

"I forgot to warn you that it will hurt—a lot," the man says, straight-faced, and I wonder if he enjoys hurting people. He seems like the type who might.

"Wonderful," says Keya. "Now we will let you get some sleep. Tomorrow is a very big day, after all. The first trial starts bright and early, and heaven knows that you of all people could use some beauty rest." She says it with a smile, though it's clearly not a compliment. "There are clean clothes in the closet," she informs me. She crinkles her nose in distaste. "You can just throw the ones you are wearing in the recycle bin."

The two of them exit my room. I remain seated where they left me until their footsteps fade away. When I can no longer hear them, I move to the door and wave my band in front of the scanner to open it. I'm not sure exactly what I plan to do next, but it doesn't matter because the door is locked.

I sink to the floor and let the cold wash of hopelessness engulf me. Never once in my life did I consider joining the Burning. The chance at a life in the Flame, with all its benefits, has never appealed to me because it's a fantasy. Keya and the Council might pretend I have a chance to pass, but it's far more likely that Oran the dragon, or any of the other mythical creatures from Dad's stories, will waltz through the door right now. It's a ruse to punish those who can't be satisfied with what life has given them.

And now here I am, in the Council's crosshairs.

The streets have mostly fallen quiet, but suddenly they erupt into commotion again.

I pull myself up and go to the only window. It overlooks the gate through which I just entered. It appears that a tall, slender guy with dark hair has just entered the Burning. I can't make out his face exactly, or hear the name that the guard announces. Something about the situation has made the people who still linger in the streets go insane.

People who had started to return to their homes now come rushing back to see what has happened. They join in the shouting as well. It's strange, but I can't make any sense of the situation.

I expect the Enforcers will be here soon to break up the disturbance. They never let something like this go on long. But the few Enforcers wandering through the crowd seem unconcerned, despite the accelerating agitation. I wonder how long they'll wait before putting an end to this.

I don't have to wait long before I get my answer. It's not shouts or the firing of a blaster that sends alarm bells blazing in my head. It's a sudden, eerie quiet, as if everyone in the streets has decided in unison to shut their mouths and go home. Silently and orderly, the streets begin clearing. As far as I can tell, nothing has been resolved. No order to end the demonstration has been issued. The Enforcers do not raise a hand. And yet, the people all move like an ancient herd of sheep.

The only hint I have as to the catalyst for the change is the wrist bands, which have shifted from black to yellow. It's strange enough that it almost distracts me from my actual worries, but not quite.

I collapse onto the bed and nestle into the warm blankets. I am exhausted. I need to sleep. But sleep eludes me. In my head, I try to recall some of Dad's stories. He used to make them up for me too, when I was little. Whyle loves stories about fairy tales where anything is possible. I always preferred stories about how the world was in the pre-Wither days. Maybe that's why I'm so fascinated by the history book I got from Kenna. But tonight, I don't need real—I need magic and hope. So I think of the stories he tells to Whyle—ones where anything, even a girl from the Smoke passing the Burning, is possible.

I wish I could believe in them now—believe the impossible. But at least I can take these stories with me to the Ash, and maybe Dad will think of them too, and they will connect us across time and space.

CHAPTER 6

Sleep finally overtakes me, but not for long.

"It's time to get up," a timid voice says, jostling me awake. A girl, not much older than me, stands near my bed looking anxious.

I groan and roll away, covering my face with my pillow.

"Breakfast is already being served," she says. "The first trial will start soon."

"Breakfast?" I whirl around and leap from the bed. I missed breakfast yesterday, and couldn't bring myself to do more than pick at lunch and dinner. The only thing I feel more strongly than despair at this moment is a deep, penetrating hunger.

"You aren't going out like that, are you?" the girl asks, genuinely alarmed.

I still haven't changed, and my clothes are the faded, filthy, thread-worn apparel of a girl from the wrong side of The City.

It's not like I have a chance in the Burning anyway, so I can't see how it matters much what I look like. Still, I might as well enjoy the amenities while I'm here, so I pull out a clean set of clothes from the closet. "Um, do you mind stepping out while I change?" I ask the girl.

She points to a door. "You can change in there while I make your bed."

I open the door to discover that I not only have my own private bathroom, but it's as large as my entire bedroom back home, and far nicer, too.

"Don't be shy about using the shower," she calls, and I take that as more than a mere suggestion.

Grime clings to my skin and mats my hair. I turn on the running water, and it comes out in a strong stream. I undress and step in. The water rains down like a gentle massage. There are several levers that dispense soaps. I don't know what the differences are, but they all smell so good that I doubt it matters. Whatever I use is bound to make me cleaner and more fragrant than I have possibly ever been.

Even though it feels nice, I don't linger. My stomach aches, and I just want to get to breakfast. I towel off and get dressed in new, clean clothes. They aren't as fancy as I would have guessed. Just a simple green shirt and dark pants, but it's still luxurious. I've never even felt fabric like this before, let alone worn it. The sensation reminds me of being wrapped in a gentle hug—not too tight, but soft, and strong, and comforting.

When I come back out, clutching my old clothes to my chest, the bed has been transformed into a decorative mound of blankets and pillows that looks more like a work of art than a place to sleep. The girl is busily wiping away at every surface. Presumably she's dusting, despite the complete lack of anything dust-like in sight. If she wants to see dust, I should show her the shelves at the market back home where they keep the luxuries too expensive for anyone to even touch, let alone buy—things like jeweled necklaces, colored paper, scented candles, and other equally useless things. I mean, who's ever going to spend twelve credits on a beaded bag to carry your stuff around in when you can make a bag out of scraps for free? Honestly, I don't know why they waste the space on these items. I suppose many of those things are commonplace here in the Flame, but they've never really been that interesting to me.

"Who are you?" I ask, not sure what's going on here, and whether she expects me to be helping her.

"I'm Petra. I'll be taking care of your room while you're here," she says, smiling.

I've never had someone wait on me, and it feels awkward. I wish she would leave, because there's something I want to do and I'm not sure if she should know. "Can you do me a favor?" I ask.

"That depends. Is it your hair? Because you desperately need some help there! If it's your hair, then I can definitely help." She looks so excited that I don't dare turn her down or admit that my hair hadn't even crossed my mind, even though it hangs scraggly and damp halfway down my back.

She leads me to the mirror and instructs me to sit. I wonder how long this can possibly take. Back home, it has never taken me more than a minute or two to brush my hair and pull the long, auburn strands into a braid or bun. Petra goes to work, complaining about the tangles but smiling and talking all the while. Then she uses a small, buzzing device to dry my hair in seconds. I hope that she's almost done with me because I really am hungry, but it seems that brushing and drying were just the prelude to the actual styling.

"What assignment are you hoping for?" she asks, pulling and twisting locks of hair.

I almost have to laugh at that, because the idea that I'll get any assignment at all is ludicrous. There's no need to point this fact out, though, so I just turn the question around on her. "Is this the assignment you were hoping for?" I ask. I'm not trying to be rude, but she casts her eyes down as though I've embarrassed her, so I add, "I mean, it seems like a really good job, to be a maid here in the Flame."

That appears to cheer her, and she smiles with a little shrug. "It's not so bad, really. I actually do kind of like it, but it's not really the most desirable job, you know."

"I would have thought any assignment in the Flame is great," I say honestly.

"Of course any assignment is great compared to being sent to the Ash, but some jobs are more desirable or more prestigious than others. Things like designers, and performers, and the Burn Masters, of course."

The Burn Master I understand, but I have no idea what those other things she's talking about are, which is probably a big part of the reason why I don't have much chance of being assigned to do them.

Her hands fall still, and I look at myself in the mirror. While we talked, she has turned my head into a masterpiece. I hardly recognize my own face, framed in flowing waves that cascade from a fountain on top.

"Beautiful," I whisper in awe.

"Not quite," she contradicts, and rifles around in a drawer, then approaches my face brandishing a small tube with a red stick.

"What's that?" I say, backing away.

"Just some lipstick. Come on, let me. It'll look great."

Hesitantly, I allow her to rub the red along the lines of my lips. The color it leaves behind has a waxy texture I can't quite get used to. I hope it wipes off.

She's reaching for something else, but I'm done. "No more," I say, standing. "I'm hungry."

"Okay, fine," she says with just a hint of a pout. "You're a million times better than when I walked in," she remarks, looking me over from head to toe. "That's what I really wanted," she whispers, as though sharing a deep secret.

"What, to make me pretty?"

"To be a stylist."

When I just stare back blankly, she adds, "They're the people who make everyone else look beautiful."

I look back to my reflection. "I can't imagine why you didn't get that assignment. You're amazing."

"The City didn't need any more stylists when it was my turn. I guess this was the best thing available at the time." She picks up a dusting wand and waves it in the air. "Not that I'm complaining," she adds quickly.

"Now, you'd better go to breakfast," she urges. "You'll need your strength today."

"Okay, thanks for everything. Just one last thing." I tuck my old clothes under the mattress while she watches in puzzlement. "Can you just leave those alone? They're the only thing I have left of home, and I'd kind of like to keep them." Even as I do it, I know it's silly and pointless, but I can't bear to part with the one last piece of home I may ever have.

She nods conspiratorially and pushes me to the door, rattling off quick directions to the dining hall. I follow them eagerly, and soon a new and strange aroma fills the air. It makes my mouth fill with saliva. The scent leads me all the way down the hallway and around two corners until I reach its source.

The dining hall is huge, and filled with at least three dozen people—mostly contestants, from the look of it. Instantly, I understand Petra's concern for my appearance. Compared to everyone else in the room, I look about as impressive as a little house made out of mud standing next to mansions. This fact appears to bother the other contestants more than it does me. I draw many openly curious glances, but it's easy to pay them little attention.

All I care about is following the red, plush carpet to the familiar serving window at the front of the room. My stomach grumbles in anticipation of being filled, and I can't help hoping that maybe they serve bigger portions here in the Flame. This is supposed to be the place of luxuries, after all. Shouldn't that include enough food to make you feel truly satisfied? What must that be like?

The woman behind the window slides me a tray. I don't even have to scan my ID band. I take it eagerly, but then pause, confused. "What is this?" The window and the tray are familiar, but what's on the tray is completely foreign.

"Your breakfast," the woman replies without humor or interest.

It doesn't look like any kind of food I've ever had, but I take it. I don't want to cause a scene with so many people watching me. I search the room for a secluded place to sit, but the best I can find is at the end of the nearest table, where I can put an empty seat between me and the group of girls sitting there.

Seated with my back turned away from onlookers, I tentatively pick up one of the brown squares and put it up to my face, inhaling deeply. This is the source of the scrumptious scent that's been taunting me. I stare at the spongy surface, still unsure.

"It's just bread. It won't bite you," a boy says, claiming the empty seat next to me.

I look up, embarrassed, to see a freckle-faced boy with red hair observing me.

"I'm Ty. It's nice to meet you," he says.

"Hi, I'm Emery," I say, and force myself to smile.

His name sounds familiar, but I can't place it. Of

course, there's no way I know this boy, or anyone here, for that matter. I wonder why he's here talking to me. I shove a bite of the bread into my mouth so I don't have to speak. The taste is so amazing that I almost exclaim, but fortunately I catch myself and keep it to an indecipherable squeak.

He smiles. "You don't have that kind of food in the Smoke, do you?"

I shake my head and take another bite, savoring the flavor. The bread is dense and thick, but somehow fluffy at the same time.

"I've heard about the meal rations you have," says Ty. "I guess it makes sense to offer the optimal nutritional balance at every meal with minimal waste. Some people say we'll go to that here soon, too."

Suddenly, I remember where I've heard his name before. This topic brings back memories of last night, hiding among sacks containing Smoke meal rations. It was the driver. He told the guard at the gate that his son, Ty, was joining this round. At the time, I didn't realize what he was talking about.

Of course, I can't tell him this little connection. I'll never tell anyone. Still, it's an interesting coincidence that the very first contestant who talks to me happens to be the son of the driver who unwittingly smuggled me across the wall. It's a small city after all.

I finish off the last of the bread and pinch a few crumbs off my tray, shoveling those into my mouth as well.

He laughs. "If you like the bread, you'll love the apple. They're my favorite."

"Why is the food different here than in the Smoke?" I ask. I crunch into the apple and experience sweetness like I've never tasted before.

"The Council says it's to conserve resources, but then why not do the same for the whole city? And besides, they claim that The City was engineered to never run out of resources, so..." He leaves the sentence hanging as though that's not the whole story, or at least he's not convinced of it.

When I don't respond, he changes the subject and goes on, apparently needing to fill the silence just like Liam. "So, what's it like in the Smoke?" he asks, loud enough that the whole table can hear him.

I shrug. "You know—dusty."

He chuckles. "Okay, then how about this. What's your family like? Do you have a brother or sister?"

"Yes, a brother," I say, and look away.

I do have a brother, but soon I might not. All because I screwed up. I was hasty and careless, and I got caught. I don't want to talk about it. Not with this stranger, no matter how nice he may seem.

The girls at the table stand, shooting curious looks our way. As they pass me, one girl with long black hair and a pinched nose speaks to her friends, but her words are clearly meant for me. "I can't wait to crush the Smoker. I hope she likes eating ash."

It's nothing more than I should have expected. It

won't do any good to get offended, so I just ignore her.

"How about you?" I ask Ty to avoid further questions about Whyle and my family.

He waits until the pack of girls has moved a few more paces off. When there's no one left in earshot, he ignores the question and leans forward, whispering, "Did you bring a message?"

"Huh?"

"Have the plans changed?"

I just stare back in blank confusion.

"Come on, Emery, just tell me straight. Has something changed? Did they send you with a message?" He looks desperate, like he's fallen into the water reservoir and is asking me to throw him a rope to keep from drowning.

My head spins from the sudden change in tone and direction. Try as I might, I can't even venture a guess at what he means.

"I don't really know what you're talking about," I admit, figuring that honesty is probably the safest response.

He locks his gaze on me, unconvinced.

It doesn't appear that he's going to give up, so I try a different approach. "As far as I know, nothing has changed." Also true—because I know nothing about what he's going on about.

He nods once, serious and resigned. "I had to at least ask, you know. I'm sure you understand," he says, then gets to his feet and marches away.

I sit there, stunned; I've never been more confused in my life.

Before I have time to try and make any sense out of what just happened, Keya—in a different but equally fire-themed outfit—starts talking from a podium that has been set up next to the serving window. Above her head, four enormous, interlocking rings are suspended in the air.

"Welcome, welcome! I am so pleased to officially begin this round of the Burning." She pauses expectantly, and the audience cheers. I manage a single, unenthusiastic clap. "This is such a special time in each and every one of your lives. And I am truly honored to be the one to guide you through this process of discovering your place among humanity."

The arrogance. She speaks as though the Flame is all that's left of human civilization, completely ignoring the Smoke and the other eleven Safe Domes.

The fervor infusing her words about this barbaric event turns my stomach. The Smoke may have its problems—and they may be far too many for me to enumerate—but we don't put everyone on display and kick out anyone who doesn't meet some arbitrary standard of acceptability. I remind myself that at least we have a choice whether or not to come. All of the children of the Flame are required to enter the Burning and prove that they have value to society when they turn seventeen.

"Today will be your Iron Trial, the first of four tests that will either prove that you belong here in the Flame of

The City, or that you are nothing but dross that must be rooted out and expelled to the Ash."

"Now, as some of you may know," Keya goes on, a somber shift in her tone, "a strange turn of events last night has left us one Burn Master short." She shoots a pointed look in my direction as a rumble moves through the room, and I'm not sure if she's looking at me or someone else. I can't imagine how she can insinuate that this has anything to do with me.

"That means," she calls over the clamor, and the room quiets again, "that we will have to make some adjustments to the way this round of the Burning will proceed. Clearly I can't manage twenty-eight contestants all on my own. So after a long deliberation this morning, the Council has decided that the Iron Trial will be an *elimination* trial."

The room erupts into chaos. This clearly means something to them that is both surprising and disturbing.

Suddenly, our wrist bands—what did Keya call them?—our *intercuffs* light up yellow. I see the glow encircling my wrist, but feel nothing. For some reason I can't explain, it does the trick, just as it did on the people in the streets last night, and the room falls into silence.

"That's better," Keya coos. "The Iron Trial will be a maze. Only the first fifteen contestants to exit the maze will proceed in the Burning. The rest will be eliminated and sent to the Ash directly afterwards."

She waits as a ripple of shock rolls through the room, then she holds up her arms in a grand gesture and proclaims, "The Iron Trial begins now!"

And the first ring above her head bursts into flames.

CHAPTER 7

Large double doors swing open. Keya directs us to proceed calmly and orderly, but her instructions are drowned in the chaos. Running, leaping, climbing, and crawling, twenty-eight terrified contestants—myself included—race for the doors, pushing and shoving as though our lives depend on it—because they do.

I make it through the entrance somewhere in the middle of the pack. Even though we're indoors, the walls of the maze are formed by some kind of shrubbery I've never seen before, growing ten feet tall, with thick, thorny, tangled branches. I only have a second to decide which way to go. It's just a random guess at this point, so there's no sense wasting time debating it. I choose the path on the right and just start running.

I remember Mom sitting at the kitchen table just last month recalling how she had to rescue a worker who had become lost in the tunnels of the water plant where she was assigned at the time. "The secret to keep from going in circles is to place one hand on the wall and follow it wherever it goes. Eventually, it will lead you through all the tunnels and to the exit, every single time."

If I place my hand on these walls, they will jab and slice my flesh and slow me down, so I just keep an eye on the wall, always keeping the one I'm following on my right. This isn't the shortest route, but it's the surest. Anything is faster than stumbling around in a confused and random path, hoping luck will lead you to the exit. Luck is a back-stabbing companion that will turn on you when you need it most. Just last night, luck feigned friendship time and again as it led me across the wall and to within inches of my goal, while all the while carefully maneuvering me into a cage.

I'm fast, and I quickly leave many of the other contestants behind, settling into a rapid pace that I can sustain for at least another hour without slowing. I pass contestants scurrying in all different directions, frantic desperation painted on their faces.

Every few minutes there's a loud crackling sound nearby, but I can't tell what's causing it, so I ignore it for now and just stick to my plan.

I run for what feels like an hour before I have to slow, but I keep up a jog. I don't know how large this room is, but I must be getting close to covering the whole of the maze. After all, how big can it possibly be?

Popping and crackling ring out from the wall to my right, and I pause and watch what happens, wondering if it's a clue to the location of the exit. I watch in shock as a section of the wall withers and the branches crumple into nothingness. What's left behind is not the exit. But it does explain why I haven't found it yet. A new pathway is now open where it had been impassable just moments before.

The maze is *changing*!

I come to a dead stop. No amount of careful strategy or speed can take me safely through a maze that doesn't stay the same. Already I may have traveled the same passages multiple times without a clue.

As I stand contemplating, the last branches of the wall recede. With it gone, I lock eyes with a guy who stands just feet away, on the other side of where the wall used to be. I don't know his name, but I remember seeing him in the dining hall. He's tall and good-looking, and seemed popular among the other contestants at breakfast. His dark green eyes hold me transfixed when I should be moving.

"It's her," he hisses to the friend standing next to him, and his features contort in malice.

"I thought we were looking for Jessamine," his companion protests in confusion.

But the angry boy ignores him. "I'm going to do us all a favor and deal with this one first," he snarls.

I stumble back and turn to run, but he leaps and tackles me to the ground.

"Come on, Vander, we're wasting time," the friend complains, though he expends no effort at all to rescue me from the assault.

"I won't be beat out by a Smoker," Vander hisses, holding my arms behind my back until I cry out in pain.

I twist and writhe, but to no avail. He's just too

strong.

The familiar crackling starts up again, and Vander yanks me to my feet. I kick and claw at him, but it doesn't stop him from dragging me to the spot where new branches and thorns are rapidly springing up to form a new wall. He pins me there as the branches twist around me, trapping me inside the wall and leaving me unable to move without ripping my flesh against the punishing, unyielding thorns.

Then Vander and his companion take off running, and are quickly out of sight.

"Help!"

Several people run by, but no one stops to free me from my prison. I suppose they're glad to see one contestant out of the running—one less threat to their own survival. I can't even blame them, if I'm being fair.

Hot tears spill down my cheeks, and I honestly don't know if they're caused by the physical pain that engulfs me or the despair at realizing I've failed the very first trial.

This is it for me.

And worse—so much worse—this is it for Whyle.

I shut my eyes against the misery.

And then crackling begins again, but this time it sounds different—slower, less rhythmic. I open my eyes to find that someone has stopped to help me. I feel the tugging away of the vines that hold me bound, freeing me from this brambly prison. They stand in the pathway behind me, so I can't see who it is, but I'm so indescribably grateful to them that the tears come again for a whole new reason.

"Thank you! If you free my arms, I can help," I suggest.

Together, we break through the branches. It's not until we've worked together for several minutes and are both covered in cuts that I'm able to climb free of the wall. I turn around and look up to see who among all the contestants has had compassion for me. I open my mouth to thank whoever it is, but freeze, mouth agape.

I am stunned speechless. I blink several times to clear my vision, sure I must be hallucinating, not merely because my rescuer is a dazzlingly gorgeous guy, but because I know him. I've dreamt of those eyes, as blue and deep as the constant sky, for years.

I don't understand how he can be here. He shouldn't be here—can't possibly be here. And yet here he stands, just inches away from me.

Eason Crandell appraises me with concern. My clothing is badly shredded, but fortunately not anywhere too embarrassing.

I haven't seen him—other than in my dreams—in two years, not since the day Raven dared me to kiss him back behind the school building. He was brilliant and funny—or so I'd gleaned from things I'd overheard him say. And while I had idealized this gorgeous guy for as long as I can remember, I'd never worked up the nerve to actually talk to him—maybe because I was intimidated by his perfection, and maybe because he is two years older than me.

Not one to lose a dare, I ran up to him, pressed my lips to his, and then ran away as fast as I could. I didn't even see his face afterward to know how he had reacted to the sudden encounter. I told myself that I would talk to him the next day, but I never got the chance. That night he joined the Burning, and I never saw him again.

And that's why he can't possibly be here now. But I'm certain it's him.

"Hi," I say, sheepishly. "Thanks so much for helping me. I'm lucky you came along."

"Yeah. Lucky," he agrees with a smile.

"I'm Emery," I say, feeling ridiculous and exposed. I never thought I would see him again, and I avert my gaze to the ground, unable to face him. "Do you remember me?" I can't stop myself from asking.

He brushes a lock of hair from my face, and I look up to meet his eyes. He cocks his head to the side, considering. "Should I?" he finally says.

I am simultaneously relieved and deflated. I don't know what I expected. I'm sure he's kissed lots of girls. I never even talked to him. And I know I wasn't the only girl who lost sleep over this boy. I wonder which of them he would remember.

I shake my head. "No, you shouldn't."

"I'm Eason," he says.

"Yeah, I know," I admit, then look away, embarrassed. I don't want to have to make any explanations on that point.

This is baffling and exhilarating all at once, but it

doesn't matter, because I come back to my senses and remember that I'm in a struggle for my survival—and for Whyle's—and now is not the time to catch up with an old almost-acquaintance. I'm about to blurt out a quick thank you and get back to running when he catches my arm.

"We need to hurry," Eason says. "I wasn't expecting an elimination trial right off. We've got to find the exit."

"Yeah…right," I stammer, a little confused at his use of the word *we*. Is he suggesting we team up? Is that even allowed? No one said it wasn't, so I'm not going to argue.

He bends down, and I'm not sure what he's doing until he says, "Climb up on my shoulders and I'll lift you up. Maybe you can see the way to the exit."

I suppose helping me might be the best way to help himself, but that's fine with me. I climb up on his broad shoulders and try to stay balanced as he slowly straightens. I start to slip and grab onto the only thing I can reach to steady myself, which is a handful of thorny briars. I recover my balance, but my hands come away with deep gouges that are dripping blood. The point of the perilous walls is probably to prevent contestants from climbing them, but neither that nor my injuries can deter me at the moment.

My vision clears the top of the maze, and I search for anything that looks like a way out. I see walls growing and shriveling in dozens of places.

"Do you see the exit?" he calls.

"I see the outer walls, but they look solid all the way

around. I don't see an exit," I report in frustration. Contestants are racing around in all directions. And then I see what we're looking for. A fast-moving girl reaches the center point of the maze, and a platform raises her into the air and out of sight. Quickly, I trace the paths from that location back to ours.

"Let me down," I exclaim. "I've got it."

Suddenly I'm free falling, and I brace myself for impact on the ground, but Eason catches me in his arms and smiles. My head is whirling, breathless from the unexpected fall and sudden rescue. He sets me on my feet, and I immediately begin running. Now that it seems possible, I want nothing more than to survive this trial, and that means reaching the center before the paths shift again.

Eason stays at my side, running in lockstep with me, matching my pace with ease. Soon, we make a final turn and enter a round clearing with a metal platform. We stand together on it, but it's really only meant for one person, so he wraps an arm around my waist to hold me steady. My heart is pounding, and I don't know if it's from the running or his proximity.

He puts his mouth close to my ear and whispers, "I knew I could trust you."

I laugh, exultant, and cling to him as we rise into the mist and reach a higher level overlooking the maze. The strange mist seems to only block visibility one-way. We couldn't see it, but everyone here can look down on everything happening in the maze below with perfect clarity.

There are seven other contestants already present. I note with satisfaction that Vander's attack on me seems to have backfired, and he is not one of the contestants that have escaped the maze. My glee can't even be dampened when I catch the eye of the pinched-nose girl from breakfast, and she makes angry snarling and biting motions toward me, as though my mere presence has turned her feral. She is definitely one to watch out for.

There are so many questions I want to ask Eason, so much that I don't understand. I'm relieved to see a familiar face—and apparently a friend. But, seconds after I arrive, Keya is at my side.

"Well done," she praises. "Though, is it really so impossible for you to keep your clothing clean and intact?" she adds in exasperation, muttering something about "upbringing" and "work cut out for me" under her breath.

I hear Eason chuckling behind me.

"It's not really my fault," I protest.

"Never mind," she says, waving her arms dramatically. "The important thing is that you made it through." She leans in closer so that only I can hear her next words. "I was secretly cheering for you, you know."

I didn't know, and can't even guess why, but it's nice nonetheless.

"Now follow me," she says, and turns and walks away.

I steal one last glance at Eason before parting from him. He smiles and winks, and I feel confident that I'll have a chance to talk to him later.

Keya sets a quick pace, and I'm not sure how she manages it in her tall, spike-heeled shoes that look absolutely counterproductive to the task of walking. I trail behind, trying to figure out how she stays upright, let alone moves as fast as lapping flames. She leads me down a hallway. Then we take an elevator to the ground floor. Soon, we enter a brightly-lit, white room with several empty beds.

"What's this?" I ask.

"The Medical Center for the contestants," Keya explains. "This is Doctor Hollen. He takes care of all the contestants during the Burning. He'll get you fixed right up."

A tall, middle-aged man wearing a long white coat comes over and appraises me. "Blazes, what happened to you?"

Keya makes her exit as the doctor leads me to the nearest bed.

"I was attacked by one of the other contestants in the maze," I tell him. "He grabbed me and trapped me in one of the changing walls. The branches and thorns cut me up and tore my clothes. And that's how I came to be here."

"I see. Well, don't worry. I'll get you healed right up. Then you can make a report about the young man who attacked you. What did you say his name was?"

"His friend called him Vander."

The doctor begins rifling through drawers in a cart at the bedside. He pulls cloths and wound cleanser from the top drawer. Then he opens the bottom drawer and removes a bottle of small white pills. It takes all my self-control to avoid reacting to the other contents of the drawer. It's filled with medicines, including several small vials labeled *Curosene*.

My foot taps with nervous energy as I wait for the doctor to finish with me. I cannot leave this room without that medicine.

"It will stop hurting soon," he assures me, mistaking the source of my agitation. "Take this pill. It will speed the healing process and stop the pain," he says after he's done cleaning the dozens of scratches, scrapes, and gouges that cover me from head to toe.

I swallow it down slowly while I consider how to get him to leave me alone. All I need is a few seconds to grab several vials.

Keya reappears just then, carrying a clean, untorn set of clothing. "I suppose we'll just have to recycle those as well," she says, referring with regret to the clothes I'm now wearing.

"Can I have some privacy to change?" I ask shyly.

I'm hoping that Keya and the doctor will leave the room for a few minutes, but they don't. Instead, the doctor does something almost as useful. He draws a curtain around me that encloses the bed and the medical cart. I'm hidden from view, and just have to make sure to not make any suspicious noise.

Focusing on the top priority, I step around the bed and carefully pull open the bottom drawer. I start shoving vials into my shoes, and they're able to hold six while still allowing me to walk, albeit awkwardly. It's painful, but that seems a small price to pay.

Then I rip off the ragged clothes and pull on the fresh blue outfit that Keya has kindly brought for me.

"Okay," I call, hopping up casually on the bed.

The doctor pulls back the curtain. He takes my hands to inspect the injuries that are already looking much better. "Be careful, now. I don't want to have to heal you every day that you're here. We're already two for two."

"Oh, you're the doctor that healed my hands last night," I surmise.

He nods.

"Thank you."

"You can go now," he says, starting to walk away.

"Wait, I need to make a report about the attack," I remind him.

He smiles. "Oh, I'll take care of it," he assures me. "You just get some rest. Everything should be all healed up in an hour or so."

Keya starts to lead me back the way we came, toward the room where contestants exit the maze, and I totter along clumsily behind her, trying to stay out of her line of sight.

"Can I go to my room?" I request as nonchalantly as I can manage.

"Don't you want to see who else survives the maze? They'll be your competition for the remainder of the Burning."

"I'm not feeling very well."

Maybe it's the shakiness of my voice, the smattering of scratches that still mar every inch of visible skin, or the way I'm limping along, but Keya doesn't push the issue further. She spins on her heels and leads us back in the opposite direction, depositing me safely in my room. I must seem really bedraggled because she goes so far as to arrange for my meals to be brought to me for the rest of the day.

"You really should take this time to prepare for the upcoming trials," she encourages.

"What am I supposed to prepare for?"

She wags her finger at me and clicks her tongue. "Shame on you. I can't go around giving contestants hints about what's coming. That would be a violation of my duties."

So basically she's telling me that I need to prepare for something, but since I have no idea what, her advice is less than useless.

Rather than fret about what's coming, I focus on the victories I just scored.

As soon as Keya leaves me alone, I pull off my shoes and nestle the vials to my chest in an embrace. This is Whyle's life I hold in my hands.

I have already passed the Iron Trial, and with Eason as my ally, maybe I can survive the entire Burning. Keya might not be able to tell me what to expect, but I'm sure Eason can give me some pointers. It's just a few days. If I can pass and get an assignment in the Flame, surely there's a way to get the medicine to Whyle. Sneaking back into the Smoke should be infinitely easier than sneaking into the Flame, and I managed that.

I am going to survive, and I am going to save Whyle and everyone who's sick.

But for now, I have to find a better place to hide the vials. I can't very well hobble around with them tucked in the sides of my shoes and squishing my toes. The vials are small, but it's like walking around with enormous pebbles in my shoes. It'll draw too much suspicion, and pretty soon they'll wear blisters into my feet.

I consider various options for hiding them in my room. I could put them under the mattress with my clothes. I check to see if Petra kept her promise and my secret; the clothes are still there. That seems like a possibility for now, but also risky. After all, Petra does know that I hide things there. I could stash them in the back of a drawer, or in the closet, but nothing really feels safe.

I'll have to keep them on me. The clothing I've been given isn't extremely tight, but it will still show lumps if I'm not careful, and there are no pockets. My body is lean and strong from years of running and hauling, but not exceptionally curvy. That limits my options for hiding this on me unnoticed.

I turn back to my shoes. They have small holes in the toes, and are well-worn. I don't really mind because it makes them comfortable. The soles are thick and sturdy, nothing like the silly things that Keya perches on with those thin little pointy heels.

But that gives me an idea, because my shoes do have slightly raised heels that are thick and wide. With effort, I pry out the insole of one shoe. When it comes out, I discover that the heel is partially hollowed. I try to fit a vial in the space, but no matter which way I turn it, the space is not quite wide enough.

I hunt around the room for something useful. The drawers near the mirror, where Petra did my hair this morning, are filled with all sorts of strange things—ribbons and bows, and clips for hair, and powders and pastes of all kinds of colors that are most likely more paint for my face, like the lipstick Petra smeared on me this morning. None of that will help me now.

The most promising thing I find is a metal nail file tucked in the very back of one drawer. It isn't ideal, but it's the best I have, so I go to work. Using its somewhat pointed end, I whittle away at the edges of the hollow space. It isn't until the file snaps under the strain that I start to make real progress with the sharp edge of one of the shards. Finally, I'm able to work it enough that three vials fit into the hollow space of each heel. I have to file away at the insole as well, until it's paper thin, before I can get both my foot and the hidden vials in the shoes at the same time.

Just as I'm about to slip on the shoes, I hear screaming and scuffling in the corridor just outside my room. Barefoot, I run to the door and listen, but don't open it, afraid of what I'll find.

"This isn't right," a terrified voice yells. "We didn't get a fair test."

What follows is a haunting cacophony—stomping, shouts, nails scratching the wall, cries of fear and pain, pleas, and the ringing sound of a blaster being fired.

Finally, the sound begins to fade, and I crack open the door and risk a peek. A dozen Enforcers are escorting—or dragging—the failed contestants away. Soberly, I shut the door on the scene. A shiver runs down my spine as I consider how easily I could have been one of them, how narrowly I escaped the Ash today. But the danger is far from over.

Whatever happens to me, I have to find a way to protect this medicine and deliver it to Whyle before it's too late. I test out walking. The heels of my shoes are now flimsy and contain fragile vials, so I walk with most of my weight shifted forward to the balls of my feet. It takes some practice and emulating Keya's posture before I'm able to maintain a reasonably normal gait. I pace around the room for the better part of an hour before I master the rhythm and balance, and walking finally begins to feel normal again. I don't stop until the clicking of my shoes on the tile sounds steady and effortless.

CHAPTER 8

Lunch is even more delicious than the bread, apple, and orange drink I had for breakfast, and so much more enjoyable in the solitude of my own room. My only regret is that there's no one to tell me the names of the foods. There's a brown, savory liquid with chunks of orange and yellow. And there is a long, yellow fruit. This morning, I didn't think it was possible for anything to taste sweeter than the apple, but whatever I'm chewing and swallowing now is so sweet that I have to alternate bites with the savory liquid in order to not overwhelm my senses.

I'm almost done when someone knocks at my door.

"Come in," I call through a mouth full of sweet mush.

Timidly, Petra enters.

"Oh, hi! Are you here for the tray?" I ask, shoving the last of my food rapidly into my mouth.

"No, I'm supposed to get you."

"For what?"

She looks away evasively. "I don't know. You just need to come with me."

I finish the last bite of food and then slip on my shoes so I can follow her.

She leads me back the way I came last night. At the exit, she holds up her intercuff to a panel next to the door and then directs me to do the same. The panel glows green, as do both of our bands, and the door swings open, allowing us out into the open courtyard.

This is the first time I've seen any part of the Flame in the bright light of day. The sight is startling, and I have to squint and shield my eyes. The blue glow of the never-changing sky reverberates off of seemingly every surface, as though the buildings and streets are all coated in a layer of crushed gems. Once my eyes adjust to the constant shifting and dancing of rainbows, my vision begins to clear.

Several buildings can be accessed from within the razor-wired, guarded courtyard of the Burning Center. Petra leads me across a long walkway to one of these buildings. Once we reach its tall metal door, we go through the same routine of scanning intercuffs that we did to exit the Burning Center. There's no sign on this building, and I get the feeling that this is a back way in.

"Where are we?" I ask.

"The Justice Building," Petra finally informs me. "Wait here. The Chief Enforcer has requested to see you."

Petra deposits me in one of the cold, metal chairs lining the walls. Work stations are placed at equal intervals throughout the center of the room. Enforcers, easily identifiable in their red uniforms with broad gold stripes over their right shoulder, bustle around. No one pays me any attention at all. I watch the seconds—and then minutes—pass on the large clock that ticks above the door through which I just entered.

I start to wonder if this is some sort of mistake, but the thought of approaching someone to ask what's going on is about as appealing as shoving my arm in the recycle sorter—not something you do if you want to remain intact.

Fourteen awkward minutes pass before a tall and heavily muscled Enforcer whose uniform bears three gold stripes, rather than the customary two, enters the room. People scurry to get out of his way as he approaches me, his face stoic and unreadable.

"Miss Kennish, follow me," he commands.

Just as I stand, another Enforcer rushes over. "Sir, I am so sorry to interrupt, but I need to talk to you," she exclaims in exasperation. "The woman is not cooperating."

I follow their gazes as both Enforcers look at a woman seated at one of the stations across the room. She has short, dark hair and a pretty face, and I would guess she's in her mid-twenties. She stares back at them as though warding off a predator.

The man holds up one finger to me, a signal to wait, and marches off across the room toward the flustered woman. From where I stand, I can easily hear their conversation.

"Hello Shawny Markum, I'm Terrance Enberg, the Chief Enforcer. Dina tells me that you're refusing to cooperate. What seems to be the problem? Do you not understand the law?"

The woman stands, and that's when I see that her belly is hugely swollen—she's pregnant. "I do understand the law, I just don't understand why such a law exists. How can you force a mother to choose between her children?"

"Of course, the Council never meant for such a choice to be required. It's for the safety and longevity of The City that the size of each family is carefully assigned. You already have your two authorized children. It was your choice to allow another pregnancy. Now you must either choose to give up the baby, or you can choose to stay with the baby in the Ash," Terrance explains in mock sympathy.

"What happens to the baby?" she demands.

The Enforcers stare back in silence.

Tears roll down her cheeks. "I can't let you take my child. I thought the entire point of the Safe Dome was to protect us, to keep us *safe*. How does this make any sense?"

"You must choose, or the Council will choose for you."

"And what about my other two children? What will happen to them without me?"

"You have twenty-four hours to decide," Terrance states flatly, and then turns back to me.

I avert my gaze, pretending I didn't watch the entire exchange. The law is essentially the same in the Smoke. Most couples are authorized to have two children—my parents, for example—but some only one, and some as many as four. I think the difference has something to do with optimizing the genetics of the population for maximum health. I've never heard of anyone being sent to the Ash for having an extra child, but maybe they just always choose to give up the baby in such a case. Parents don't get any extra credits to support unauthorized children, so it's too big of a strain on the whole family for anyone to risk.

Terrance turns to the other Enforcer. "Dina, please get started with Miss Kennish, and I will join you momentarily. I've just remembered that I have a quick bit of business I have to attend to."

She nods and turns back to me. "All right Emery, shall we?" She gestures for me to follow her back into a private room.

She shuts the door behind me. The room is small, with nothing more than a table and three chairs. She directs me to the closest chair and seats herself on the opposite side of the smooth, wooden table.

"It sure is a surprise to see you here," she says jovially, which is incredibly suspicious.

"Yeah, not many of us join the Burning," I mutter.

"It's always fun to see the contestants from the Smoke try so hard in the Burning, as though they have a chance. I'll admit, there have been a few who made it through. But really, I don't know why any of you come at all." The friendliness melts into mocking.

I keep my mouth shut and my eyes fixed on hers. She's clearly trying to provoke or scare me for some reason, but

I'm not taking the bait.

"Let's be honest with each other for a moment. Can we do that?"

"Sure," I reply, not sure at all.

"How did you get here?"

"I joined the Burning," I reply, trying to hold my voice steady.

"Oh, don't be coy with me, Emery. You may have fooled Enforcer Dickens, who found you, but we know the truth. You never scanned your ID card to officially cross the Wall of Fire at the Burning gate. So how did you come to be in the Burning?"

I'm sure it's too much to hope that if I admit to everything, she'll let me out of the Burning—let me go home. More likely, I'll just be sent to the Ash immediately. Surely entering the Flame illegally would disqualify me from earning an assignment in the Burning. I can't think of anything that I can say to help my case, so I keep my mouth shut.

"Your performance so far is fairly impressive," she muses. "It really is a shame that you won't get to complete the Burning."

This time, she's the one who waits for me to respond.

"What do you mean?" I ask, trying not to let my voice shake. "I passed the first trial. That means I get to stay." It's really not fair to make me go through all of this if they never intended to let me finish.

"Normally it would, but that's for people who are law-abiding citizens, not liars and thieves."

Suddenly my shoes—concealing Whyle's only hope of survival—feel like red-hot coals strapped to my feet. Though my stomach tightens and my mouth goes dry, I summon every ounce of strength I have to remain impassive. "What do you mean?"

She slides a tablet towards me and taps it. It shows several scenes—me exiting the courier truck, me slinking through the dark streets, and finally, me being apprehended behind the Medical Center. "What were you planning on doing?" she demands.

My mind spins desperately to grasp any possible explanation that doesn't involve attempted theft.

"Do you have kids?" I ask.

"Yes, two daughters," she admits, unsure where this is going.

"I bet you and your daughters get along really well," I say, trying to sound both admiring and mournful.

An involuntary laugh escapes her lips. "Not always, but I fail to see what this has to do with anything."

"Well, I'll tell you. I actually wanted to join the Burning, but my mother wouldn't let me. She just doesn't believe in me. She was watching the gate on our side of the wall. I knew she would stop me and I would miss my chance." As the words escape my mouth, I can't help being a bit impressed with my ability to weave this fabricated tale so quickly.

She looks like she's buying my story, so I layer it on thick, even though merely pretending a love of the Burning is nauseating.

"I just happened along the courier vehicle whose Enforcer was chasing down some guy who had stolen a sack. I thought it was my chance to follow my dream of joining the Burning. I slipped inside the back of the truck and got across the wall."

"That doesn't explain why you were wandering around the Flame. When Dickens caught you, you were all the way over at the Medical Center, a long way from here."

"Well how was I supposed to know where to go? It's not like we have maps of the Flame back home," I answer quickly. It's true enough that I didn't know how to reach my intended destination. I'm not telling her anything she didn't already know, except for my objective. This is the only motive that can't possibly get me into any more trouble.

Her face is regretful. Maybe she can imagine one of her own daughters doing something similar, and I begin to think she's inclined to extend some amount of mercy, but then she starts to talk, and her words hold no sympathy.

"Those who earn a place on this side of the Wall of Fire are the best, smartest, and purest of humanity. There are many benefits to living here, but they must be earned, and they must be guarded. You have already shown that you lack the moral character required of a citizen of the Flame. No matter what the reason, the laws and order of The City must be maintained. The City is a carefully crafted, complex system, and to ensure our survival, every piece must function flawlessly. The penalty for illegally entering the Flame is exile. There is no point in you continuing in the Burning. You will be sent to the Ash immediately."

She stands and exits the room, and all my earlier hope is effortlessly reset to zero. Her one kindness is to leave me unobserved as I sink into despair.

CHAPTER 9

I'm not sure how much time passes in the small gray room, or how many buckets of tears I spill before the door opens again. I wipe my face dry with my sleeve and turn to see who has come for me. Terrance Enberg, the Chief Enforcer, saunters in.

"Please," I cry, "I didn't mean to cause any problems." It's probably a lost cause, but maybe he has some compassion. What can it hurt to try?

He stares at me for a long moment before speaking, and something in his expression looks almost pleased. "I do understand," he says, sitting and reaching for my hand as if to comfort me. "I really do want to help you. Will you let me help you?"

I nod, unsure where this is leading, but grateful that I may at least have a chance.

"I could make it so that your past indiscretions are completely removed from all record. That would mean that no further punishment would be necessary, and you could continue in the Burning and have a chance to prove yourself worthy of the Flame."

"You could do that?" I ask, sure that there must be a pretty big catch.

"I could," he hedges. "But in order for me to help you, I need you to help me."

I can't imagine what he could possibly want from me.

"Will you help me, Emery?" he prods.

"I can try."

He claps his hands. "Excellent. It's not a lot that I ask. All I need is for you to befriend one of the contestants and get some information from them."

I think of the stares and jeers I got this morning in the dining hall, remember my terror as Vander attacked me, the threats breathed out by the black-haired girl as she left the breakfast table.

"What makes you think anyone will talk to me?"

"I think you're the perfect person for this assignment. I'm positive that if anyone can find out what's going on, it's you."

I can't guess what would make him think that, but there's no sense arguing the point if it's my only chance to stay. "What information do you want?"

"We simply need to know what it is that this particular contestant hopes to achieve in the Burning."

That doesn't sound so difficult or dangerous, just asking someone what assignment they hope to get. I don't know why it matters so much, but what can the harm be? And what choice do I have?

"Okay, I'll do it," I agree.

He smiles like we're old friends. "I knew you were a smart girl." He places a tablet on the table. "Here's the boy who's about to become your new best friend." He taps the screen, and my stomach drops as Eason Crandell's face appears.

*   *   *

I bury my head in my pillow to stifle a scream. It's almost impossible to believe that just twenty-four hours ago I sat at Whyle's side, just inches away from my mother and father. Despite the disastrous turn of events over the course of the last day, I cannot lose sight of why I'm here—the only reason I'm here. Not for me, not for Eason—for Whyle.

I could accept being sent to the Ash if only there were some way to get the medicine now in my possession to Whyle first. That's all I really care about, but I desperately don't want anyone else to get hurt in the process.

I pull myself together enough to stand and cross to the window. I spend some time observing the outer yard of the building, but I don't see anything to bolster my hope. The prospect of me escaping from the Burning is slim. In addition to the razor fences and guards, I now wear an intercuff which surely tracks me, they've shown that everything is monitored, and I have now drawn the particular attention of the Chief Enforcer—which almost certainly means that the Council is involved somehow, too.

The five men and women of the Council who run The City are the ones who pass final judgment, deciding which of the contestants ultimately pass the Burning and what their particular assignments will be.

I'm sure they're monitoring my every move. That means that my best chance of escape will come after the Burning is over, when I'm free to move about the Flame. Maybe I can even get an assignment, such as a courier, that will give me legal access to return to the Smoke. But to have any chance at all, I must not only pass the Burning—something pretty unlikely—but I must also satisfy Terrance Enberg's demands. Both feats will require Eason's help.

I want nothing more than to hide in my room for the rest of the evening and eat the food Keya already arranged to have sent for dinner in solitude, but I know that would be a dangerous move. Before releasing me, Terrance made it very clear that he expects me to get results fast, so I must at least appear to be trying.

Nerves rattled, I make my way to the cafeteria. I collect my tray from the window and look around to choose a seat. I'm one of the first contestants to arrive for dinner, and I have my pick of the tables. With nearly half of the contestants eliminated this morning, it's not going to get crowded.

I consider claiming a table alone and waiting for Eason to show up. But just as I'm about to take a seat all by myself, Ty walks in. I don't want to give him the opportunity to corner me and ask more incomprehensible questions. A repeat of this morning's confusing conversation is the last thing my mind can handle right now. I steer clear of the pinched-nose girl and wander over to an empty seat across from a girl who looks like she might be friendly, and at the very least, probably won't try to bite me.

She looks up and smiles at me, which is a good start.

"Hi, I'm Emery," I say.

"Jessamine," she says, introducing herself.

Jessamine—the girl that Vander and his friend were looking for in the maze. I don't know what they planned to do when they found her, but I immediately feel a kinship with this girl.

"You're from the Smoke, right?" she asks.

I nod.

"What made you decide to join the Burning?"

"Oh, you know, hope for a better life and all that," I mutter, distracted as I glance around the room. Eason hasn't shown up yet, but I spot Vander heading right for us. I grab Jessamine's arm, and she jumps in alarm.

"What is it?" she asks.

"Vander is coming. Jessamine, he was looking for you in the maze."

"Really?" she asks, and turns to smile at him.

"No, Jessamine. I don't think you understand. He's dangerous. He attacked me. I almost didn't make it out because of him. I don't know what he was going to do to you."

She ignores me and stands up, waving him over. When he reaches her, he holds his tray in one hand and wraps the other arm around her waist. Then I watch, aghast, as she rises to her tiptoes and gives him a kiss.

He lets go of her and sets his tray on the table across from me. That's when I stand to leave, grabbing for my tray, but Vander's quick and he catches my wrist. I rip it away, prepared to yell for help.

"Don't go," he implores. His voice is gentle. Even the shade of his green eyes has lightened and softened away from the gloom of the maze.

I'm so stunned that I just freeze and stare at him, not sure what to think.

"I wanted a chance to apologize about earlier," he says, and he seems genuinely contrite, locking me with a pleading gaze.

Stupidly, I start to get a little lost in his pale green eyes. I turn away from his bewitching gaze and focus on taking a deep breath, reminding myself that Vander is dangerous, and if I let my guard down, he will strike.

"Come on, sit down," Jessamine says.

Slowly, I resume my seat, but I'm not at ease.

"I just want you to know that I didn't mean for you to get hurt earlier," he says in a pretty convincing imitation of sincerity. I suppose whatever report the doctor made led to him being reprimanded in some way, which certainly serves him right.

"You could have fooled me," I reply. "If it weren't for Eason coming along and being a decent human being, I'd be in the Ash right now, thanks to you."

"I really am sorry. I can't even explain what possessed me to behave that way, but I can assure you that I will not harm you again. I am truly sorry." His expression is pleading and repentant, and I would like to believe him.

That's when I see Eason finally appear and take a seat a few tables over.

"Fine, Vander. I guess I forgive you," I say as I stand and pick up my tray. "You'll have to excuse me now."

As I leave, my seat is claimed by the boy who was with Vander in the maze.

"Hey Jasper," Jessamine greets him.

"What are you talking to the Smoke girl for?" Jasper asks in a poor attempt at a whisper. "I thought you said…"

Vander cuts him off. "I shouldn't have said whatever I said."

I don't hear the rest of the conversation as I pass out of earshot, which is fine with me. I cross the room and claim the seat next to Eason. The minute he looks at me, all the weight I'm carrying—every worry and responsibility—feels lifted.

It would be best for Eason if I just stayed away from him. Maybe it's selfish, but I want to be with Eason. Not because of Terrance. Not because of the Burning. Just because of Eason. I wish that such a distinction were actually possible. He is my one consolation in everything that has happened, and I'm just not strong enough to deny myself that.

There must be a reason why Terrance needs a spy to gain this information from Eason, and a reason Eason wouldn't want to share it with him. So since I can't stay away from Eason, I settle for a promise. I promise myself that, no matter what it costs me in the end, I will not betray Eason. I just have to appease Terrance so I can stay. Surely I can find a way to do both—shield whatever secret Eason carries while feeding Terrance and the Council a plausible falsehood that protects us both.

"I don't think that I said a proper thank you earlier," I say.

"I don't think I said a proper you're welcome." He runs his fingers through his dark hair, tousling it. "You look better," he says with a smile.

I've been so distracted that I completely forgot about my myriad of wounds, but my arms and hands are perfectly healed now, and I assume my face is, too.

"That's good stuff that the doctor gave me." I wonder how many credits medicine like that would cost us back home, if we could get it at all.

His eyes linger on my face just a little too long, as though he's trying to figure something out. I realize that when he saw me in the maze, my appearance was marred. This is the first time he's seen me as I usually appear—minus the fancy hairstyle.

I feel my cheeks flush, and I take a bite as an excuse to turn away. "Mmm, that's good," I exclaim.

He laughs. "Mashed potatoes are one of my favorites."

I study him for a moment, trying to puzzle out questions of my own. "Can I ask you a question?"

"Sure."

"I thought only seventeen-year-olds could enter the Burning."

"So what's your question?"

"Haven't you already been through the Burning?"

"Yes." He meets my gaze as he says it, as though he's trying to convey something more than the single word, but I don't know what.

"So how is it possible that you're here now?"

"Are you disappointed to see me?"

"Not at all. It's nice to have a face from home," I admit. *And a gorgeous one at that*, I think but manage to not say aloud. Still, the fervor that escapes in my tone has me blushing all over again.

"You have no idea," he muses. "I've waited a long time for a friend to come along."

"But that doesn't explain how you can possibly be a contestant now."

"I joined again. Anyone who has previously passed the Burning can re-enter at any time if they want to receive a new assignment."

"But then, don't you also risk failing and being sent to the Ash?"

"Yes," he says, and I can't imagine how he can sound so unconcerned about it. Even if he passed once before, there's no guarantee he can do it again.

He's looking at me like he wants me to ask something more, but I realize just how dangerously close we are coming to discussing the very thing that Terrance wants so desperately to know, so I change the subject.

"What's the one thing that you miss most about home?"

"My mom," he says.

"Yeah, she was worried after you left," I recall. Because it's so rare for anyone to enter the Burning, it's pretty big news, and it doesn't take long before everyone knows about the contestant and the family they left behind. Of course, I had my own reasons for being aware.

That catches his attention. "You know her?" he asks excitedly.

"Only a little," I admit.

In the Smoke, we pretty much all know each other a little bit. Everyone has worked with or eaten with just about everyone else at one time or another. Between frequently changing assignments and eating times, we have a casual relationship with everyone, but deeper relationships are rare. I can't help wondering if that's just a sad side effect of the system, or actually the point of it.

"How is she?" he asks.

"Like I said, she was really worried when you left. The Enforcers had to make her come to meals, even." His brow furrows at this revelation. "But I think she's doing well now," I assure him. "The last time I saw her, she was helping a new mom and her baby."

He smiles. "She's always helping someone," he muses. "I've worried a lot about her. I wish I could see her or talk to her. I didn't want to leave her, but it's what my father wanted."

That surprises me. "I thought your father died," I say, hoping that isn't insensitive. "I just remember you and your mom."

"It was just us, ever since I was a baby. But we both knew that this was what he wanted."

I'm not sure what to say to that.

He seems to sense the awkwardness and decides to shift the topic, again. "You seem to know a lot about me and my family," he observes, his eyes betraying amusement.

"Yeah, well, I saw you around," I say casually. "Like everyone, you know."

He nods seriously. "Of course, like everyone."

"But you don't remember me at all?" I challenge.

He smiles. "Well, I have seen you around. You know—like everyone in the Smoke."

I sigh. While the thought of that kiss is mortifying, it's also insulting that it didn't merit one single spare memory cell.

"Of course," he adds, placing a hand on mine, "you don't forget a face that beautiful."

My breathing hitches and my heart does a little back flip. I savor the feel of his warm hand on mine, not daring to move for fear he'll take it away. I suppose I can forgive him. He had more important things on his mind that day, like throwing his fate before the mercy of the Council.

I take a few more bites, savoring the flavor, and I can't help noticing that he seems to appreciate the food just as much as I do. We eat in silence for a few minutes before I finally work up the courage to ask him a vital question. "Eason, can you help me with something?"

He nods. "Sure, what do you want?"

"What do I need to know to pass the Burning? You must know a bit about how to survive it."

He smirks as though I've said something funny. "A bit."

"So what do I need to know? What's coming next?"

He considers for a moment. "Did you know that the Wall of Fire and the Burning were not part of the original design for The City?"

I shrug, not sure what this has to do with getting me through the Burning successfully, but I humor him anyway. "Yeah, sure. The Wall of Fire went up eighteen years ago. Anyone who wanted to live in the Flame had to earn their position by undergoing the Burning. Those who didn't want to risk it had to live in the Smoke."

He nods. "Did you know that not all of the Council members agreed with the Burning?"

"No, I didn't know that," I admit. "But it doesn't seem to matter much now, does it?"

"It might matter more than you think."

I wait for him to expound, to tell me how this is supposed to help me, but when he speaks, he has switched topics once again. "Did you know that the architect who designed the Safe Domes never actually made it to the shelter that they offered?"

Again, I don't know why this matters, but it is interesting. It's not something that we learned about in school in the Smoke, but maybe it's common knowledge here in the Flame.

"No, I didn't know that. What happened?"

"No one's really sure. With each version of the barrier field, he made enhancements. Ours was one of the last— number ten out of twelve, to be exact. Some people think he was going to build another one. Some people think he contracted the Withers, and so he couldn't be admitted into a Safe Dome."

"So he's dead?"

"I didn't say that."

"Look, Eason, this is fascinating, but I don't see how this helps either of us make it through this round of the Burning, unless you're planning on joining the architect as a Roamer or a corpse," I complain.

He smirks and rolls his eyes. "Fine, you want to know the secret to passing the Burning?"

I nod eagerly.

He leans forward and motions for me to do the same. "Meet me at breakfast tomorrow, and I'll tell you."

CHAPTER 10

When Petra comes to clean the room in the morning, she finds me sitting in front of the mirror, angrily attacking the knots in my hair with a brush.

"Stop that!" she commands. "You're going to rip your hair out, or break the brush. How did you manage to make such a mess of things?"

She holds out her hand for the brush, and I relinquish it to her superior capability. The rhythmic stroking of my hair is soothing, and somehow she works out all the knots without pulling my hair.

"I guess I tossed a lot during the night. I had nightmares." All night, the Burning, Terrance Enberg, and Whyle's lifeless corpse took turns inflicting their own forms of torture on my unconscious mind.

"That's understandable," she consoles.

I close my eyes and relax as she begins to style my hair into something not just presentable, but stunning. I smile, anticipating seeing Eason again.

"What's the hardest part of the Burning?" I ask. Any information I can get about what's coming can only help me survive.

"For me, it was definitely the Bronze Trial. I was never the best at my studies, even though I tried hard enough. Things just don't really seem to stick. But I managed to squeak through, apparently."

She launches into a long story about a book that she had to read in her last year of school. "I swear I read that thing ten times over and I still couldn't pass the test. I guess that's the one good thing about being assigned as a maid—no tests." She pauses, and her brow furrows as though she's considering something unpleasant. "It really is a shame that you decided to come here right when you did. I've never seen a round of the Burning with so many eliminations. In my round, there were only six people who didn't make it all the way through and receive an assignment. I guess I'm lucky. And of course, usually no one is sent to the Ash until after the Refinement—which is the ceremony where the results are revealed and those who pass receive an assignment. No matter how badly you do on any one trial, you usually get four chances to prove yourself."

"In the four trials?"

"Exactly. I've never seen an elimination trial before."

"But why is this round different? I don't really understand what's going on."

"There are supposed to be two Burn Masters to help all the contestants and oversee all the trials. Keya can't do everything on her own," Petra explains.

"But what happened to the other Burn Master?"

Petra's hands freeze in my hair, and I wonder what I've

said wrong. Am I not supposed to ask about this? "I have to go," she says, dropping the brush into my lap. My hair is lopsided, with the right half done up in beautiful curls and the left hanging limply like a drowned rat.

"What do you mean?" I ask in disbelief. "What about my hair? I can't go around looking like this, and I can't do anything with it on my own."

She holds up her right wrist; her intercuff is now glowing yellow.

"What does that even mean?" I demand.

She picks up the basket she entered with and rushes for the door, despite the fact that she hasn't done a single thing to clean the room since she entered. "Yellow is a warning. It means you've broken a rule. I've been in this room too long, neglecting my other work. I have to go."

"Wait," I beg.

She pauses, and the light of the band shifts to orange. Her body tenses for a moment, her brow contracts, and she groans.

"Did that hurt?"

She nods, gritting her teeth. "Yellow is just a warning. If you don't obey the warning, pain starts with orange."

Hastily, she exits the room.

I scramble to my feet and follow her out into the hallway. A few people are walking by and give me strange sidelong glances, probably owing to my barefoot, bedraggled state. I ignore them and run to catch Petra before she enters the next room.

Her band has stopped glowing, but she doesn't seem

eager to upset it again.

"How many colors are there?"

"Yellow, orange, red, and then blue."

"What happens when it turns blue?"

"It'll knock you unconscious after a few seconds," she says.

"The pain is that intense?" I ask in shock.

She nods once, her eyes hollow like ghosts, and I can't help but think that she has experienced this before.

*   *   *

"Nice hair," Eason comments, and I honestly can't tell if he's admiring or mocking me.

Back home, I would just leave my hair down in natural auburn waves that hung halfway down my back, or pull it into a bun to keep it safe from machinery, depending on where I was working. But Petra was right yesterday about needing to do something with my hair in order to fit in. Every girl has elaborate, beautiful, and sometimes eccentric hairstyles. After I lost my hairdresser this morning, I had to do the best I could on my own. I managed to twist it up on top of my head and pin it in place, which hides the fact that only half of my hair is curled.

"Thanks," I mutter back. "You don't look so bad yourself," I add, and it's true. He has adapted well to the Flame and their perfectly manicured styles in the years he's spent here. "So what do I need to know?" I ask in a hushed tone, getting straight to the crux of the matter.

"The most important thing to remember is that none of this is about you—what you know, what you can do." He leans in and keeps his voice low. "It's all about the system. All the Council really cares about is preserving the system indefinitely."

I don't really understand how that's supposed to help me with anything, but I try to remember it all the same. "But what do I need to *do*?" I press. "Can't you give me something more specific?"

He spears a bite of an orange fruit and waves his fork at me, shaking his head. "Not now. Just eat your food." Disappointment must be evident on my face, because he adds in a gentle tone, "It's all going to be fine, Emery. Just trust me."

I want to trust him, but I don't know how with so much at stake. Ultimately I'm at his mercy here, so I agree to be patient. As I eat my food—which is distractingly amazing—I notice that all the other contestants sit in groups of four or five, and they all seem to be sitting as far from us as possible. Many of them sneak furtive glances our way.

"Do they really hate us so much just because we're from the Smoke?"

Eason rolls his eyes. "It's not you, trust me," he says, twisting his mouth into an ironic half-smile that reminds me why I had an insane crush on him for so many years. Who would have thought that the first real conversation I would ever have with him would be on this side of the

Wall of Fire?

"What makes you think they like me any better than you?" I counter.

"Well, how many riots have you caused this week?"

It takes me a second to realize what he's talking about. "You mean the other night, when all those people were in a frenzy down in the streets, that all had something to do with you?"

He stands and reaches his hand out to me. "Let's go for a walk."

I let him help me up, and his grasp is warm and steady. He leads me from the room, and I feel like I can breathe better, free of all the oppressive gazes and malevolent stares. We scan our bands at the door and exit into the courtyard.

"Are we allowed to be out here?" I ask.

He taps his intercuff. "It wouldn't open the door if we weren't. It's not like we can go anywhere."

We follow a paved path that circles a green lawn, and I don't know if I've ever seen anything so vibrant and alive.

We walk in silence for several minutes, passing Enforcers every few yards. A few other contestants start to wander around the grounds as well. He leads me to a wooden bench in one corner, as far from the path and Enforcers as possible.

"So what was the riot all about?" I ask when we're alone and seated.

"When I joined the Burning, the news spread pretty fast. Some people started to panic."

"Why? Is it that unheard of for anyone to try for a new assignment?"

"Not really. It happens maybe once a year or so. Usually it's a maid or a courier who has studied and prepared and believes they can get a better assignment if they try again," he explains—which actually explains nothing about the people's panicked reactions.

"I still don't understand. Why did people care about *you* rejoining, then?"

"It's not so much *me* as my previous assignment that scared them."

"So what were you?"

"Haven't you guessed yet?"

And then it clicks…

"The second Burn Master." It seems so impossible that a boy from the Smoke would be assigned to such an important role that I never even considered it.

He inclines his head, confirming my speculation. "I didn't anticipate the Iron Trial becoming an elimination trial. That was an unfortunate side effect. I guess people did have reason to be worried."

My hand flies up to my mouth. "Oh, no! It's your fault that all of those other contestants had to go to the Ash," I whisper, horrified.

"I doubt it. Maybe the exact way it worked out was my fault, but remember what I said about the Council. They wouldn't let go of anyone that they believed The City needs. The same number of people were going to be cut no matter what I did, I'm sure of that much. And with the way that maze kept shifting, they had a lot of control over who made it through and who didn't. I think they just presented it that way to make me look like the villain here."

"Would they manipulate it that way?"

He shrugs. "Why wouldn't they? They can't leave something that important up to chance."

If that's true, that explains one reason why the Burning is so notoriously impossible for people from the Smoke. But then, why did they let me through at the expense of one of my Flame-born opponents?

"Why give up your position, Eason? If the Burning is as controlled by the Council as you say, then it seems like way too big of a risk."

"It's what my father wanted," he states flatly.

"Your father?" I huff in exasperation. "How in the world could you know that if he's been gone since you were a baby?"

"It is. Trust me," he says with complete confidence.

"Eason, that doesn't make any sense. You were safe. You shouldn't have come back."

He appraises me for a long moment, seeming to consider what to say next. He opens his mouth to speak, and it occurs to me that I've inadvertently allowed the conversation to drift to exactly the topic that Terrance seeks to understand: what Eason's purpose is in coming back to the Burning. If it were something he was inclined to tell the Council himself, they wouldn't need me to spy for them. And the only way I can ensure that I won't betray him is if I have no information to betray him with.

Before he can utter another word, I leap to my feet and start walking away.

"Emery, wait. What's wrong?" Eason calls after me, racing to my side.

I don't stop walking. "It's just that my shoes are bothering me." It's completely true, but utterly beside the point. My altered shoes dig into the soles of my feet in awkward places, and I give in to the urge to limp, which makes my excuse to leave extremely convincing.

"You should get new ones."

"With what credits?" I ask, suddenly annoyed. I start back for the door to the building with Eason trailing behind.

Jessamine is sitting alone on a bench. She smiles and waves as I approach. Then Vander runs right by her, and neither of them acknowledges the other at all. I wonder if something happened since yesterday to come between the happy couple. I wish Vander would ignore me as well, but as he runs past us, he takes the opportunity to kick dirt in my face. I cough and spit in his direction, but he's already out of reach.

So much for apologies.

Eason and I don't speak until we reach the door to my room.

"I'll see you later," I say, anxious to hide behind the heavy wooden door. This is all so complicated. I just want to be alone. And I do, in fact, want to take off these blazing shoes.

He looks alarmed, probably sensing that he's upset me but understandably confused as to how. He reaches for my hand. "Emery, I really am glad that you're here."

"Why, Eason? What does it matter to you if I'm here?" I demand, trying to figure him out. I need him, but I can't imagine why he could possibly need me. As much as it pains me to admit it, even to myself, he would be a lot better off if he had just passed me by in the maze, like everyone else.

He drops my hand and looks away. "It's just that I've been waiting for…"

"For me?" I ask, incredulous.

"Not exactly. But I'm glad it is you."

We stare at each other for a moment, both trying to read something in the other's eyes and both coming up blank.

Finally, he backs away, and I shut the door, taking refuge in the solitude of my empty room. I peel off my shoes and sink into the softness of the bed. But my reprieve lasts only a few minutes before my intercuff flashes, and white letters appear on the surface.

Report to the trial room for your Bronze Trial.

I slap my forehead and moan because I didn't get any more information from Eason about what to expect next, and now it's too late. And I'm annoyed that he didn't just tell me when we had a chance at breakfast. After all, he hasn't just been through the Burning before—he basically *was* the Burning. If he's so glad to have me here, then why isn't he working harder to make sure I can stay?

I take a deep breath, roll from the bed, slip my feet back into the torturous shoes, and head off to face the trial that Petra claimed was the worst of them all.

CHAPTER 11

I sit in a small cubicle, barely the width of my arm span in either direction. The other contestants are all in cubicles just like mine right now, closed on the four walls, but opened to the ceiling so that Keya and a dozen other people I don't know can look down from the raised platform and observe us, just like they did in the maze trial, though this time they aren't hidden behind a layer of haze.

I can't imagine how they have so completely transformed this space—from green shrubbery to simple cubicles—in less than a single day. Workers must have been busy all through the night to accomplish the task.

Craning my neck, I gaze up and wonder which of the observers are members of the Council. I've never actually seen any of the five men and women of the Council. What reason could they ever have to come to the Smoke? In fact, I don't even know their names and never cared much about them until incredibly recently. Still, it's impossible not to have felt their presence on a daily basis, even if I never gave it much thought. Everything in The City—from the formula of our food rations, to our work assignments, to the granting or withholding of vital medications—is determined by the Council and implemented by everyone else with almost a graceful precision.

As far as I know, the Council has consisted of the same five since The City began. If one needed to be replaced, the assignment would be made through the Burning. That hasn't ever happened, to my knowledge. Of the onlookers gazing like gods from above, only one—a silver-hair man who looks equal parts arrogant and exhausted—looks old enough to be on the Council, but I have no way of knowing if he actually is. It seems irresponsible to make such big decisions about our lives with only one person to observe all the contestants, but the Council must be very busy.

Above us, Keya begins speaking, her voice reverberating around the massive room. "Welcome to the Bronze Trial!" she proclaims with utter satisfaction.

The rings that hung above her in the dining hall when she announced the start of the maze have now been moved into this room, where all the trials take place. They hover in the center of the room at the same height as the raised platform which hugs the walls. The first ring still burns, and at her words, the second ring bursts into flames as well.

"In a moment, the screen before you will light up and you will be presented with questions to test your knowledge on every subject of importance," Keya explains. "You will have two hours to complete the trial. Good luck!"

The screen on the wall is the only thing in the cubicle, other than me and the uncomfortable chair I'm seated on. With nervous anticipation, I watch as the screen flickers to life and words appear along with a keypad for me to type my responses.

It gives me a fairly easy history question to begin:

What was the original Wall of Fire?

Confidence bolstered, I start typing:

A ring of fire that burned for a month to prevent Roamers infected with the Withers from approaching The City during the time that the barrier field was being assembled. The area that was burned is now the Ash.

The borders of the screen flash green, and a new question appears. It is a mathematical calculation. Already, I can see why anyone from the Smoke is unlikely to pass the Burning. I solve it without much difficulty even though it pressed the limits of everything I've learned in school. If it weren't for the books that I bartered from Kenna at such a steep price, I would already be struggling.

At first, I feel fairly confident in my answers and am rewarded with mostly green flashes as the questions move from one to the next. But as I progress, the minutes pass, and my nerves tighten, my responses come slower and with less surety. My answers are met with an increasing number of red flashes. I have no idea how many answers I'm allowed to miss and still pass, and it's impossible to keep count anyway.

Just when I think I've made it through every possible

subject matter, I groan in exasperation as a new kind of impossible query is presented.

If a doctor is treating two terminally ill patients—one child and one adult—who each need the same treatment to be cured and the resources are only available to save one of them, which one should the doctor choose?

There is such little information given that I have no idea how I'm supposed to decide. The only factor that distinguishes them is their age. If that's all I know, then shouldn't the doctor save the younger patient, who has more life ahead of them?

But what if the older patient is a better person, kinder, smarter, braver, a parent to children who love and need them? Doesn't that count for something?

Maybe the doctor should choose at random, giving each person an equal chance at survival.

I rub my temples and try to think. There has to be a logical, clear answer. But these are not the kinds of things we learn in the Smoke. Our schooling doesn't deal with the theoretical or philosophical. It's all processes and procedures so we can do the tasks we'll be assigned, not how to make moral judgments about them.

In fact, I'm pretty sure that if a question of who lives and who dies were necessary, it would be left up to the Council to decide.

Yes, that must be the right answer.

Whichever patient the Council approves for treatment, I type, and anticipate the green light in response.

But the screen flashes yellow for the first time, and

new words appear. *You must decide.*

After a moment, the same question reappears, awaiting my response.

"Blazes," I exclaim under my breath.

Aggravated, I can't help wondering how Eason managed to score so well his first time around. He's in a cubicle of his own, possibly answering the exact same questions, but I can't imagine they pose much difficulty to him now. I grind my teeth in frustration. Eason must have known that this was coming. He must have expected that I would struggle with it. In fact, without knowing about the contraband books I've studied, he should have assumed I would fail completely.

Couldn't he have told me one single thing?

But then something clicks, and I realize that he did tell me *exactly one* thing, and maybe that was the best help he could give. There really wasn't time for him to teach me advanced mathematics, or tutor me on the entire process for bioengineering food. He may not have told me *what* to answer, but he told me how to *think* about my answers, and that may be enough to tip the scales in my favor.

I fight through a fog to recall exactly what he said.

The most important thing to remember is that none of this is about you. It's all about the system. All the Council really cares about is preserving the system indefinitely.

And then I'm positive I know the answer.

I begin to type. *The doctor should save the patient who is capable of providing the most continued value to the survival of The City as a whole.*

The screen flashes green, and a new question appears.

*   *   *

My bare feet are cold and clammy against the tile floor as I walk lines next to my bed—back and forth, back and forth. It's shocking how quickly a habit such as pacing, which you'd long ago dispensed with, can reassert itself under the proper duress.

The result of today's trial will be posted in the dining hall later today for everyone to see. Keya said that this is the only trial whose results are publicly reported. I keep trying to stay calm. Pass or fail, there's nothing I can do about it now. I'm not sure if it's out of fear or hope, but my feet and hands just won't stay still.

A hard, mechanical rapping sounds at the door to my room, and I jump. A very unwise flutter of hope rises; perhaps Eason has come to check on me—to pass the uncertain time together.

I cross the room and open the door with a smile, which quickly fades.

Terrance is standing in the hallway. Without waiting to be invited in, he pushes past me and strides into the room.

I shut the door and turn slowly to face him.

"Why aren't you taking this seriously?" he demands, his dark gaze boring into me.

"What do you mean? I did my best," I stammer. "It's just that most of the questions aren't things they teach us in the Smoke."

He scoffs. "I'm not talking about the *trial*. I'm talking about our *deal*."

"But I have been trying. I ate dinner with Eason last night, and spent the morning with him. It takes time to get him to trust me. I asked him about the Burning, and why he came, and…"

He breaks through my stammering. "And when he was starting to open up to you, you decided that your feet hurt so bad that you had to flee."

That knocks the wind right out of me, even though I shouldn't be surprised. Hadn't I known that we would be watched? Still, this confirms my suspicions beyond a doubt. Nothing we say or do is private.

"I… My feet did hurt."

His face contorts in rage. "Forgive me if I find the delicate flower routine a bit hard to swallow coming from you. I get the feeling that you don't appreciate the gift I'm offering. Not only am I wiping clean your past indiscretions, I'm saving you right here and now."

"What do you mean?"

"You just failed the Bronze Trial. No less than I would expect from an ignoramus from the Smoke."

My heart sinks. I had really started to think I had a chance. But there was truly never any hope. "If I failed then I'm going to the Ash anyway, so what's the point of our deal?"

His smile returns. "That's what I'm telling you. You're no good to the Council if you've given up. Technically you just failed, but I have the power to change that. It's a simple matter, really. But I need to know that you're going to do your part—whatever it takes."

There isn't one reason for me to trust this man and his promises. I could do everything he asks—betray and endanger Eason—and he could still throw me to the Ash. Who could or would stop him? But if I don't convince him that I'll try, then Whyle might as well already be dead, because I will never get the Curosene back to him.

"I understand. Thank you," I say, the words tasting bitter on my tongue. "I won't let you down."

He's standing near my bed now, and he reaches into his pocket and pulls out a small, round object. Then he turns and, holding his outstretched hand over my pillows, squeezes and crushes the sphere. A gray powder pours from inside. Then he tosses the broken ball carelessly over his shoulder, and it falls in scattered bits across the tile floor as I watch in confused shock.

"See that you remember that," he says, rubbing his hands together to rid himself of the remnants of the powdery substance. Then he marches to the door, exiting without another glance in my direction.

Hesitantly, I approach and put a finger to the gray powder soiling my beautiful bed. I look at it closely and raise it to my nose, inhaling to ascertain what this is. But, of course, I should have known.

Ash!

This is a warning.

I tear the covers from my bed and throw them in the

corner of the room. Then I curl up on the mattress and try not to panic. My breathing is coming too fast, too irregularly. I make myself inhale and exhale, and I count my breaths.

When I reach three hundred and eighty-four breaths, another knock sounds. Perhaps Terrance has thought of more ways to intimidate me. I stand and cross the room. At least I can breathe, and my legs aren't shaking as I open the door, braced for another round of threats. But the hallway is empty except for a box resting on the floor just beyond the threshold.

I pick up the box made of beautiful, sturdy recycled paper and bring it inside. The box alone is one of the nicest things I've ever been given. I wonder what could be inside. When I pull off the lid, a brand new pair of shoes awaits me. They are sparkling silver and come up high around my ankles for support. The heels are higher than my old shoes, but sturdy. I've never seen such a flawless pair of shoes, let alone owned one. At first, I think that Keya must have noticed my outfits were incomplete and sent them, but then I see a scrap of paper tucked into the bottom of the box.

> *I had a few credits to spare and thought maybe these would help. You'll need them for what's coming.*
> *—Eason*

I slip the shoes on, and they are a perfect fit. I'm not used to people paying attention to the little things I need. All my life, I've just taken care of my own problems, and it usually works out just fine. My parents counted on me to not need anything—and so I don't. Whyle tries—or tried—to look out for me, as much as a little boy can. Still, it feels foreign to accept help from someone else—again.

It feels strange to need help.

And even stranger to like it.

CHAPTER 12

When it's time to go for dinner, where our results will be revealed, I consider wearing my old shoes, even though they are about as comfortable as walking barefoot across rubble. The thought of leaving them unattended in my room—with the precious medicine that they conceal—is too big a risk to take. But then, not wearing the clearly superior shoes that Eason gave me would demand questions that I do not want asked. Nervously, I tuck the old shoes under the bed and wear the blissfully comfortable gift.

I'm one of the last contestants to enter the dining hall. There is a large screen above the serving window now, but the results of today's trial are not yet displayed, leaving the room humming with anticipation.

"Oh, I love your shoes," Jessamine observes as she stands behind me in the line for food.

Awkwardly, I try to find a way to return the compliment. It's not as though Jessamine, with her beautiful golden hair, sparkling necklaces, and easy smile is difficult to compliment. It's more that anything I say only highlights the sad contrast between the two of us in starker detail. I'm not used to feeling so self-conscious, but something about this place has that effect on me.

I'm saved from the necessity of saying anything when Vander comes from across the room and wraps an arm around her. "I'm sitting right over there," he tells her, pointing to a table in the corner.

"I'll be there in a minute, Van," she replies, nestling her cheek against his.

He gives me a friendly wave, then departs.

"I thought you two were fighting or something," I say.

"What makes you think that?" she asks, confused.

"This morning I saw you two pass each other in the yard outside, and it looked like you were ignoring each other."

She glances away. "Sometimes he's just really focused on running," she explains, suddenly intensely interested in the trays being served at the window.

Eason is already seated in what has quickly become our usual place. After accepting my own tray, I make my way over to sit with him.

"Thanks for the shoes," I say. "It was really nice of you." For some stupid reason, my voice breaks a little on the last few words.

"I was glad to do it. You deserve something good for once." His gaze is penetrating.

Dinner tonight is more of the bread and the brown, chunky liquid that Eason tells me is called soup. I can feel Terrance's gaze settle on me from across the room, and I know that I have to keep a conversation going.

"Eason, tell me about the Flame." This is a safe topic,

and I expect there'll be lots for him to tell me, so it should fill the time nicely.

But I'm disappointed.

"It's sparkly and stifling," is all he has to say on the matter.

"Well, surely there's something you like."

He lifts a spoonful of the soup. "The food is top-notch," he concedes, and chews with exaggerated satisfaction.

"So none of this is worth it?" I ask, discouraged.

He frowns and shakes his head. "I'm sorry. I probably sound pretty cynical. There are a lot of great things about the Flame. Passing the Burning means you'll have all the credits you could ever want, plenty of food, the best medical care, and constantly be surrounded by beauty. It's a nice life. But I guess I'm a little jaded after years of not only watching, but being a participant in the system that tells good people that they just aren't enough, aren't needed, aren't wanted. Sometimes it's just too much."

"So that's why you want a new assignment?" I whisper. If that's all it is, I can't see what all the fuss is about. Honestly, couldn't the Council guess as much themselves?

"Not exactly."

And I know that Terrance will want to shoot a blaster right through me, but I turn back to my food and very pointedly do not ask for clarification.

"Can I have your attention?" Keya calls from the podium where she addressed us before the maze. She looks like she's positively bursting with excitement. "The results are in, and I must say that you all have done very well. I am so proud of...well...most of you," and she beams in satisfaction, as though she personally had anything to do with our performance. "Gather round," she calls, gesturing for us to all come forward.

The room erupts into chatter and the squealing of chairs sliding across the floor as we all get to our feet and move forward. After my conversation with Terrance I already know that the board will reveal that I've passed the trial, so I shouldn't be nervous, but for some reason I can't explain, my knees shake as I walk.

Eason puts an arm around me to steady me, and I relax. "It's going to be fine. I promise," he whispers into my ear as we wait for the results to appear.

I cringe slightly at his words. It might be alright for me, but even if I never tell Terrance a single word, does he know how much attention he's drawn from the highest levels? Will he be okay? I can't imagine why they care so much about this boy from the Smoke.

"We will now reveal the scores." Keya raises both arms above her head, and the scores appear.

Fifteen names are ranked on the board from highest to lowest. There's no indication of how we actually did on the test, only how we did in comparison to one another. I scan with a single focus and find my name on the ninth row—a safe and unassuming middle score. I wonder where I would have fallen if Terrance didn't want something from me.

Menacing glares are flung my way from all directions.

Even Jessamine looks angry. I guess there was no harm in being nice to me when it appeared I didn't have a chance. Anyone who bothers to spare a glance for me now appears livid, all except Eason, who looks openly impressed. My face burns in embarrassment. I'm the only person who can ever know that I deserve neither the malice nor the admiration this score has earned me.

I scan the list for names I recognize, which is less than half of them. It doesn't even make me uncomfortable that I can't match most of the names to the faces around me. Why would I want to make friends or get close to any of them? And how will it help me to know whether, for example, Gaven is the tall guy with spiky black hair, the stalky boy with freckles, or the olive-skinned guy who's always got his arm around a girl, but rarely the same one twice? Blazes, Gaven might even be a girl's name for all I know, and I can't see how that would matter either, so I don't waste my time or energy worrying about names. If someone's important, I'll figure it out soon enough.

Jasper—the boy who was with Vander in the maze—comes in first. I guess what he lacks in spine and moral character he makes up for in brains. Jessamine is in fourth, Ty sixth, and Gaven—whoever that is—ranks tenth, just above Vander. With some selfish satisfaction I see that the pinched-nosed girl, whose name I have actually learned is Mieka, is ranked fourteenth.

And Eason is *dead last*.

I turn to him in horror, but he doesn't look concerned.

"What happened?" I demand. "How is that possible?" There's no indication of what ranking is required to pass. Does this mean that everyone passed? Surely Eason—the prior Burning contestant and former Burn Master—could not have failed.

My pleas for an explanation are drawing unwanted attention, and he takes my hand and leads me away from the throng, not stopping until we reach the empty hallway.

"Eason, tell me what just happened," I cry. The thought of him in the Ash is too terrifying to consider. "Tell me that's a mistake. It can't be right."

He places both hands on my cheeks, holding my face and forcing me to look at him, to focus. The blue current of his penetrating gaze calms me. "It's okay, Emery," he says in a soothing cadence, and he is so calm that I can't help but believe him.

"But what does this mean?" I ask, mollified. "Did everyone pass?"

"There's really no way to know for sure how the Council will consider your performance until the Refinement," he says. "There's no exact standard of pass or fail, even though we all talk about it that way."

"But you did the worst of everyone?" I confirm, still confused.

"Yes," he says, still unconcerned.

"And you're okay with that?"

"Yes," he replies, a hint of triumph in his tone that scares me.

CHAPTER 13

In the morning, dark circles betray the unslept state of my eyes. Terrance and the Council are right to suspect that Eason has a motive of his own for being here. I'm worried that whatever game he's playing, whatever he thinks he might accomplish, is going to end with him in the Ash. That thought is as painful and terrifying as imagining myself there.

I face a terrible paradox. Somehow I must protect him. But how can I protect him when I don't know what he's doing? And I must not know, because the only way to ensure that I cannot betray him is if I have nothing to betray him with.

Dazed, I sit in front of the mirror waiting for Petra to come and make me look Flame-worthy, but when she comes in, she's all business and gets right to making the bed with little more than a hasty, "Good morning," mumbled in my direction. She doesn't even ask for an explanation of the pillows and blankets piled in the corner of the room.

"I'm so glad you're here," I say. "I need a friendly face. I thought someone was going to poison me last night after they saw that I didn't totally fail the Bronze Trial."

"Your score was impressive," she agrees—to which I cringe for having deceived her with the altered score, whose only real purpose is to allow me to continue to be Terrance's pawn.

"Can you help me with my hair again? We can do something quicker today," I assure her.

She's already gathered up yesterday's laundry and the recycle bin.

I wonder if she's mad at me, too, but she looks genuinely regretful when she says, "Not today, Emery. Sorry. I just really have to focus on my work." And with that, she's gone just moments after she arrived.

I wonder if it's just the intercuff she fears, or if she's gotten into any more trouble for how much time she spent helping me over the last few days. I really hope not.

I stare at the mirror and try to figure out what to do. I've never cared so much about how I look, and I know it's not Keya or the Council that I care about impressing. I manage a decent enough braid and decide that will have to do for today. Then, on a whim, I pull out the tube of lipstick and do my best to apply it the same way Petra did. The first attempt leaves me looking like I've sustained some sort of gruesome injury in the general area of my mouth. Annoyed, I wipe it off on the inside of my sleeve and make one more attempt. This time, I'm very careful and deliberate to keep the color only on my lips. The result would make Petra proud—or at least, I don't think she would grimace. I briefly consider trying out some of the other colors for my eyes and cheeks, but decide against it.

When I exit my room, I'm pleasantly surprised to find Eason waiting for me, casually leaning against the wall. He takes my hand, and we make our way to the dining hall. It's odd that I've only been here a few days and already I feel my life settling into a pattern that almost feels comfortable—meals with Eason, carefully crafted conversation, walks around the grounds. If it weren't for the constant trials and threat of the Ash that hangs over my head and keeps reasserting itself, I might feel almost happy here.

At breakfast, I sit with Eason in what has become our regular spot, but I do my best to keep him talking about inconsequential things that veer well clear of any dangerous subjects.

"What did you say this is called again?" I ask, spearing a slice of purple fruit and devouring it with delight.

"A plum."

"Where do they grow all the food?" I wonder. "I don't think it's in the Smoke."

"Come on, I'll show you," he offers, standing.

I get to my feet and follow him. As we walk, he takes my hand. I can't help but notice Keya's gaze following Eason from afar, and I get the distinct impression that her disappointment in his recent course of action is not merely professional.

"Eason," I begin as we exit into the courtyard, "were you and Keya ever…something?" I ask sheepishly, not sure how to phrase my question, and not sure that I want the answer.

"Would that matter?" he asks playfully.

A knot forms in my gut, and I hate that it does matter to me. The thought of Keya and Eason standing together on the upper-level and presiding over the Burning, stealing kisses in the corridors, and laughing over dinner together is nauseating.

He leads me to a small glass building around the far side of the yard, an area that I haven't been to before.

"She's very pretty," I observe, trying to sound detached.

"Very," he says, nodding in agreement.

"So, how long were you two together?"

"Two years," he says casually.

Involuntarily I turn to him, eyes wide. "Two years!" I exclaim, hating the agitation that seeps into my voice despite my attempts at nonchalance.

"Yes, we worked together as Burn Masters ever since I passed the Burning two years ago," he says innocently, but he's suppressing a smirk.

I groan at his not-so-funny joke and give his shoulder a playful nudge, but a part of me wants to smack that smug smile off his face. He's torturing me just for fun.

"I can tell she likes you," I say. "I see the way she watches you."

We pause outside the door to whatever this place is that he's brought me.

"Maybe," he admits. "Keya is great, but there's never been anything romantic between the two of us. But I will tell you, Keya is one of the good guys. Don't forget that, in case it's ever important."

I have no idea what I'm supposed to do with that information, but as long as there has never and will never be anything between the two of them, I'm happy.

He opens the glass door to the small building. I start to walk past him, but he puts his arm across the door frame, forcing me to stop right in front of him.

"You know, you're cute when you're jealous," he says, clearly enjoying this.

I scowl at that and push past him through the doorway. "I'm not jealous," I insist, but his laugh informs me that I'm not as convincing as I hoped.

Gazing around the place he has brought me to, I freeze, transfixed, all thoughts of Keya forgotten. The room is small and the walls are made of glass, allowing the warm skylight to filter inside. Rows and rows of plants grow in stacked planter boxes bearing fruits and vegetables in every conceivable color. Vines twist and weave their way up lattices. Along the far wall, trees no taller than my shoulders are laden with fruit.

"What is this place?" I stammer in awe.

"The greenhouse," he says, looking around at the foliage and multicolored fruits with reverence. "This one is just for the Burning Center and the Justice Building. There are twelve of them in the Flame."

"Are we allowed to be in here?" I ask, suddenly worried. I'm not going to destroy my chances to pass the Burning and save Whyle just so I can appease my curiosity.

"Sure," he says with a shrug. "It would be locked if we weren't. And don't forget these." He holds up his wrist to display his intercuff. "It's pretty clear here when you've broken a rule. Food isn't rationed so strictly in the Flame. That's one of the main perks."

I relax and inhale deeply. The air is sweet, and there is a tangible feeling of something so vibrant and energizing here, as though the plants exhale the very essence of life itself. "I've never seen anything like this before."

There's so much food, and yet it doesn't seem like nearly enough in this one room as small as my bedroom back home.

"There are just twelve of these greenhouses?" I ask. "How fast does the food grow? It doesn't seem like that would be enough food for everyone in the Flame."

"It's not just the Flame," Eason explains. "Even the meal rations for the Smoke are based on the components of live-grown food. There are some recycled components, but not the bulk of it."

"How is there enough for everyone, then?"

He lets the question hang in the air, offering no explanations or suggestions. After a few moments, he plucks a long, thin, red fruit from one of the plants and offers it to me. "Want to try something new?"

"Definitely," I say, reaching for it eagerly.

He pulls it away with a mischievous smile. "I warn you, this is not like anything you've tried."

Now I'm incredibly curious. Everything I have tried so

far has been incredible—and all of it is like nothing I tried before the Burning.

He relinquishes it into my outstretched hand. The surface is smooth, almost like plastic. I pull it up to my lips and open wide, anticipating what new taste I'm about to experience.

He holds up his hand. "Just a little bite."

I take just a nibble, and its flavor is slightly bitter, but still good in its own way. Eason's watching me, expectant. I'm about to take a second taste when something changes.

"How did they turn fire into a food?" I demand, my burning tongue hanging out as I fan it, but the cool air does nothing to quench the pain.

Eason laughs. "It's called a pepper, and it just feels like its burning. It won't harm you, I promise. I did warn you that it's not like anything you've tried before."

"How do I make it stop?" I complain. I would expect this kind of treatment from Mieka or even Vander, but not Eason.

"Here, bite this." He plucks a yellow fruit from one of the tiny trees, removes a section of the outer peel, and hands it to me.

Eagerly, I sink my teeth in and tear off a big chunk of the juicy fruit. But instead of the delicious sweetness I've come to expect of such things, sour erupts in my mouth, so intense that it involuntarily contracts all the muscles of my face.

"What are you doing to me?" I cry.

"That's a lemon. Very sour, but what do you notice

about the burning sensation?"

I swallow, and as the sour clears, the pain recedes as well. "It's better," I admit in astonishment.

"Emery," he says, suddenly intense, "sometimes we think the worst thing imaginable is the lemon, and we'll do anything we can to avoid the sour. But sour won't hurt us, and it can wipe out the fire."

He's trying to tell me something important. I don't know what it is, and I just want him to stop. This greenhouse must be monitored. Terrance is probably watching us right now, analyzing every word we're saying.

I want to tell Eason to stop, to warn him that the Chief Enforcer is watching him, but doing so would seal my own fate and ensure Whyle's death. So instead, I take a careful step to my left and knock over a bucket filled with small, green pellets. "Oh, I'm sorry. I guess I'm a little clumsy in new shoes." I bend down and start cleaning up the mess.

Eason works alongside me. Close to the ground, hidden behind walls of plants, he looks like he's about to say something else, so I crawl away from him under the guise of looking for stray pellets.

Finally, the bucket is refilled. We stand and brush soil from our knees.

"I need to go and change before Keya sees me like this," I say.

He nods, looking a little deflated. "That's probably a good idea," he agrees. "The Silver Trial will start before long. I'll see you there."

As I retreat to my room, I wonder if I'll ever have a conversation with Eason that doesn't end with me making excuses and awkwardly running away.

CHAPTER 14

The third ring, representing the Silver Trial, is now ablaze above our heads. Once the final ring is lit and the Gold Trial complete, it will be time for the Refinement—the ceremony in which judgment is passed and our fate irrevocably decided.

This trial is different than the last two. We've all been brought into the trial room, which has been transformed again. Half of the room has been partitioned off with a thick curtain, behind which I can't even imagine what awaits me or what could require these flimsy gowns that we've all been forced to wear. The guys especially look ridiculous, but the gowns aren't flattering on anyone. I steal a glance at Eason across the room and amend my assessment—he looks good in anything, apparently.

The contestants are being called back behind the curtain three at a time, and the rest of us sit in chairs that have been set up in rows. We've been assigned seats, and Eason and I are separated by eight other contestants. I wish I had asked him what to expect, but I'd been too distracted with fire fruit and trying to save Eason from his own need to tell me things he shouldn't.

I find it odd that there's an extra chair, but then I

realize that there are only fourteen of us present—one contestant is missing. Even though I don't really know most of them, it doesn't take me too long to ascertain the absence of the only contestant with ember-red hair and know that it is Ty who has failed to show up. He was a little unstable from the very first morning here. I wonder if he's starting to crack under the pressure and decided to skip this trial. I can't imagine that would be allowed. Certainly, it would seal his fate in the Ash. Or maybe he made other arrangements for this trial somehow. Everyone here has some kind of connection that I lack.

Even though we haven't been instructed to remain quiet, a heavy feeling settles over the group, and no one says much as we wait.

Jessamine is part of the first group called back. She's joined by Gaven—who it turns out is a boy, the one with freckles—and a girl named Winter. I recognize her as one of Mieka's friends, which is an automatic strike against her in my book.

When I realize that the seating arrangement is also our testing groups, I groan. I'm seated next to a mousy girl named Ashlyn, who I have no problem with, and Vander, who I just can't seem to escape no matter how hard I try.

"This is the easiest one," Vander says, leaning over so he can keep his voice low.

"Huh?"

"You look worried, but the Silver Trial is the easiest one. I mean, not necessarily the easiest to pass, but you don't really have to do much."

I have no idea what he's talking about, but then our names are called and I figure that I'm about to find out.

The previous three contestants don't return to the group, so I hope that when my turn for whatever this is comes to an end, I'll be allowed to go back to my room. We make our way behind the curtain and find Doctor Hollen waiting for us.

"Take a seat," he instructs, gesturing to the three metal exam tables behind him.

Ashlyn claims the closest one, Vander the next, and I climb on the farthest one. My gown does little to protect me from the cold, which slithers its tentacles up my spine and around my limbs.

Vander's words make sense now. This trial is not a test of our ability, but a test of our health and vitality. I feel vulnerable and exposed. It's bad enough that Vander is here, but I also can't ignore the appraising gazes of the people looking down from the upper level, and I wonder with trepidation just exactly how thorough this exam is going to be.

The doctor is efficient as he draws blood from each of us in turn, collecting it in tiny, clear tubes.

"Next, come over here," Doctor Hollen instructs, directing us to stand on some kind of strange machine—one for each of us. The base is a rectangular strip, and there are bars to hold on to. He places a band around my head and another that encompasses my chest, then he does the same to Vander and Ashlyn. When he's finished, he pulls out a tablet and taps a few buttons. Shockingly, the floor beneath my feet begins to shift. Not the floor, really, but the machine I'm standing on. I yelp and start walking to keep from being thrown right off. The others do the same, but without the surprised exclamation.

"What is this?" I ask.

"It's a treadmill," Doctor Hollen explains. "The bands that I just placed around you will monitor your vital signs and brain function under physical strain to assess your strength and conditioning."

I almost have to laugh at whoever came up with the idea of a running machine. I wonder if this is used exclusively for medical exams, such as this one, or if this is something that many people have here. Who would want to expend so much effort just to stay in one place when there's so much you could accomplish and so many places you could go with that time and energy? Perhaps here in the Flame, with easy assignments and things like cars to drive you around, exercise is something that you have to do for its own sake because life is just too easy. I'm not entirely sure how I feel about that.

I try to settle into a rhythm, but the speed keeps increasing every few seconds. Still, I easily keep pace with the machine. I'm very glad to be wearing my good shoes today. Eason was right about that, so I guess he did help me on this trial, after all.

Once the treadmills have reached their peak speed, Doctor Hollen excuses himself for a moment and leaves the three of us to continue running alone—if you don't count our overhead audience leering down at us.

"Why don't you sit with us anymore?" Vander asks, and it takes me a second to realize that he's talking to me, not Ashlyn. She looks a little surprised as well.

I don't know why he's being so friendly today, but I don't trust him. I want to just ignore him, but I can't keep myself from laughing. "Why, so you can throw food in my hair, or trip me as I walk by?" I wonder if his whole purpose here is just to distract me during the trial.

His brow furrows like something I've said upsets him, but he doesn't deny it. "Eason is trouble. You should really stay away from him," he says instead.

"I'll take my chances," I snap back, but with a twinge of guilt. Maybe the dirt in my face yesterday was an accident and it's me who's being petty and mean. But I don't really think so. I just can't figure him out.

"Hey Ashlyn, are you okay?" he asks in concern, noticing how pale she has become. Her breathing is coming in gasps now, much more labored than it should be from the exertion of running.

She shakes her head and covers her mouth like she's trying not to vomit, and she looks like she might collapse at any moment.

"Dad!" Vander yells, but he keeps running.

At his call, Doctor Hollen comes running.

Great! So that explains why Vander has been friendly since we've been here. He's the son of the doctor, and I guess he's putting on a good show for Dad. I suspect that also means that the report about the attack that Doctor Hollen promised to make never actually happened. Still, someone overlooking the maze must have witnessed it, right?

The doctor pulls out the tablet and uses it to bring Ashlyn's treadmill to a stop. She immediately slumps to the floor and rests her head on her knees. Doctor Hollen offers her a pill and directs her to place it under her tongue. The relief is instantly visible on her face.

"Thanks," she mutters. "I'm just so nervous about everything."

I watch all of this without breaking stride.

"Why don't we finish up with you first so you can go lay down in your room?" he offers, leading her away. "You two just continue until I return," he calls to us over his shoulder.

I could go on jogging for much longer at this pace without difficulty, so I'm not concerned that he's left us here. I steal a glance at Vander and smile when I see the beads of sweat pouring down his face and soaking through his exam gown. He's breathing hard.

The doctor leads Ashlyn behind a curtain, and soon a mechanical hum fills the room.

"What assignment do you want?" Vander pants as we wait for our turn.

"You can conserve your energy better if you don't talk," I reply.

He falls silent, so I guess he got my not-so-subtle hint—though I'm actually doing him a favor by getting him to stop wasting oxygen. He should be grateful, but when I look over at him, the dejected expression on his face and the downturn of his pale green eyes assaults me with waves of shame.

I groan. "I don't even know what my options are," I admit. "I just need to pass."

"Don't we all," he muses, his thoughts clearly elsewhere.

"How about you?"

"Honestly, I don't care. Any assignment is perfectly fine with me."

I wonder if he's just saying that so that he won't be disappointed if he doesn't get what he really wants, or if he's a believer that whatever is best for The City is best, period.

Soon the doctor returns. We fall silent, and he waits for one of us to either give up or for our bodies to give out. Vander is panting hard. It takes a while, but finally he stumbles and is unable to regain his footing before the treadmill sweeps him off the end. With an awkward hop, he barely manages to keep from falling. But he's off the treadmill, and it comes to a stop.

"All right, that's it for you," Doctor Hollen says. I can't tell from his expression if he's pleased or disappointed in his son's performance. He's clearly perfected his stoic professional face for situations like this.

I'm breathing hard, but it's nothing I can't handle for a while longer. I'm surprised because I thought that the kids in the Flame trained for the Burning. Even if they didn't know the exact tests, I'm sure every one of them has been preparing for a test of their physical fitness. They might have treadmills of their own that they run on to practice. But it seems that no amount of manufactured exertion can train you better than the rigors of real life.

I run in peaceful silence for a few more minutes until the doctor returns for me. A painful stitch is forming in my side, but I know I can push through it. I go for a while longer, but Doctor Hollen and the onlookers from above are starting to look bored and annoyed. Finally, I give in and let myself stumble off the machine.

Even though I've chosen to stop, and I'm expecting the transition between the running belt and the ground, my feet just don't manage to adjust fast enough. I take a tumble even worse than Vander's, knocking my head hard against the floor, and everything goes black.

*   *   *

When I awake, I'm lying on an uncomfortable bed, and the thrumming noise from earlier is nearby. I'm looking up, and it takes me a minute to realize what I'm seeing because I'm not used to staring at the back of my own head. A three-dimensional projection of myself—inside and out—hovers above me in the air. The doctor taps several buttons on a machine, and then the image disappears.

"All right, Emery, that is all," Doctor Hollen announces. "You have completed your Silver Trial and are free to leave."

I sit up and rub my head where it impacted the floor,

but it feels fine now.

I want to ask how I fared in the trial. What does my blood sample and body scan say about my value to The City? But I don't think that's something he can divulge right now. I remember Keya saying that the Bronze Trial would be the only one for which we would receive our ranking.

Still, I can't help feeling confident that, whatever else the tests might show, I can run circles around any of the other contestants, and that must count for something.

CHAPTER 15

A blaring siren penetrates my sleep and rips me back to wakefulness. It's just as well to be free of the torture my dreams were inflicting on me. Bleary-eyed, I sit up and try to figure out what's going on. It's not until my intercuff begins to glow yellow that I think to check it for instructions.

Report to the dining hall.

I stagger down the hallway, joined by a few other stragglers.

When I arrive, the main hall is full of contestants, Enforcers, maids, nutrition workers—seemingly everyone in the building is in this room. The screen that previously showed our Bronze Trial results is now displaying a broadcast from what looks like the interior of the Justice Building.

Terrance Enberg comes into view on the screen, and my heart starts palpitating at irregular intervals. "Citizens of the Flame," he says. "I regret disturbing you at such a late hour, but a grave situation must be dealt with immediately."

He gives a signal, and two Enforcers approach, hauling along a guy in handcuffs. Even though his head is down and his face shrouded, I know immediately who I will see when Terrance grabs a fistful of the boy's red hair and pulls his head up to face the camera.

Ty.

A gentle hand envelopes mine as Eason claims the space next to me.

"Ty Pierce was apprehended this evening in the midst of an attempt to travel without authorization across the Wall of Fire, from the Flame into the Smoke," Terrance explains. I guess that explains his absence from the Silver Trial this morning, though I can't imagine why he would do this. Was he that afraid he would fail the Burning, even after ranking sixth on the Bronze Trial?

"The order of The City must be maintained for the safety of all," Terrance goes on. "This is not the first of such infractions by citizens in recent days." As he says this, I know he must be referring to me. "While in the past the punishment was expulsion to the Ash, the Council fears that the delicate balance that creates the life-sustaining system of The City is being undermined. For this reason, the Council has seen fit, in its wisdom, to elevate illegal crossings to the status of an unforgivable offense for which no degree of leniency can be shown."

The camera turns to the wall, and we hear the punishment administered as the Enforcers' blasters ring out—not the high pitch of a stun blast, but the low whine of a kill shot. Then the screen turns black.

Shaking, I shrink into Eason's side. He puts an arm around me and pulls me close, allowing me to bury my face in his neck and stifle a scream.

Quickly, Eason leads me toward the door. Of course, this means something more to us—the only people here from the Smoke, where Ty was attempting to go—and people intuitively move out of our way, letting us pass.

It's more than just that, though. In my gut, I know that this was my fault.

I let Eason guide me, and it isn't until he pulls me through an unfamiliar door that it occurs to me that I don't know where he's taken me. For a second, I think maybe I was disoriented and he's actually brought me to my room. Then I notice that the mirror is in the wrong place, and I realize that this must be his room, not mine.

Once sheltered inside, I collapse in on myself, sinking to the ground in a heap. It's not just Ty and the gruesome brutality that they made us witness. How am I supposed to ever get back to Whyle if that's what I'm up against? That could have been me. Maybe it still will be, because even now I know I'll risk anything to save my brother.

"They... They... They killed him!" I shout. "I thought the entire reason for the Safe Dome, The City, the Council, all of it, was to keep us *safe*."

Eason sits and pulls me over next to him, wrapping me in his protective embrace and letting me soak his shirt in my tears.

"It's my fault, Eason. This wouldn't have happened if it weren't for me."

"How can this have anything to do with you?" he asks, trying to soothe me.

But I can't tell him the whole truth. There are too many things I can't explain—about Whyle and stolen medication and a deal to decipher Eason's secrets. Not when the long tentacles of Terrance's surveillance could have followed us even here, to the solitude of Eason's room.

Eason runs his fingers through my hair, gently stroking my head, and lets me cry until my tears and strength are exhausted.

It's only then that I am able to speak at all, and I tell a lesser truth. I explain Ty's bizarre questions at our first meeting. "I didn't know what he was talking about, and he wouldn't leave me alone. I assured him that as far as I knew, nothing had changed. I should have been more direct with him. That must have had something to do with this. I just don't know what he thought I knew, or what he was trying to do."

"He may have been part of the Resistance," Eason speculates.

This is only the second time I have ever heard of a Resistance, both times since crossing the Wall of Fire.

"What is that?"

"Well, it's nothing, technically. No organization. No leader. But the Council believes there's a growing faction, particularly in the Smoke—though not exclusively—that is unhappy with the way The City runs. Some think they want to leave, others think they want to overthrow the Council and bring down the Wall of Fire. It's not like they've ever made any formal demands, because technically they don't exist, and that's why they can't be caught or stopped."

I listen in fascination. "And you think Ty was a part of that?"

"I don't know, but I bet the Council thought so."

"I've never heard anyone talk about a Resistance in the Smoke," I admit. I can't imagine that any rational, sane person would actually *want* out of The City. No matter how imperfect things may be inside, it's far better than anything we can hope for beyond the barrier. "I don't believe it actually exists."

Eason says nothing, but he chews at the inside of his cheek. He seems to be contemplating something, but says nothing for a long interval.

I lean my head on his shoulder and relax into the silence. It feels nice, calm and safe. My eyes close and I start to doze, when suddenly he shakes me awake. He puts a finger under my chin and pulls my face up to look at him. He gazes into my eyes, searching for something. I stare back, completely open to him.

"Do you trust me, Emery?" He's serious and somber in a way I haven't seen before, and I'm certain that if I say yes, he'll tell me everything that I need to give Terrance to save myself.

Of course I trust him. More than that, though, I am in awe at the trust he seems so willing to place in me. I want so badly to know what makes him confident and self-assured, and fearless. But for his own protection, I can't let him say it. And even if that wasn't the case, in this moment, I don't care what he wants to say because I'm so overcome by the mere fact of his presence and his regard for me.

I push myself up and press my lips to his.

The kiss only lasts a few seconds, but it's enough to make me feel like I'm floating, like time has frozen and the two of us fill the entirety of the universe. Nothing else can matter, because nothing else exists except Eason and me in this moment.

"Who did you lose a bet to this time?" he whispers when I pull away.

The spell is broken, and I go rigid like a statue. "It was a dare," I say stupidly, as if the distinction matters.

"Oh, my mistake," he says with an exultant smile.

"Why didn't you tell me that you remembered?"

"Because it didn't seem like you wanted me to. I figured that if you were willing to risk everything to cross the Wall of Fire, you deserved a fresh start, if that's what you wanted."

"It was stupid of me to take that dare. I'm sorry," I say with chagrin.

"I'm not. That was the one moment I actually regretted my decision to join the Burning. You almost made me reconsider."

"Really?" Even though I want to, I find that difficult to believe.

"Really," he replies with no hint of deception or mockery.

Hot shame washes over me. I can't keep playing this

evasive game with him. He has to know the truth about Terrance, and the Council, and their intentions for our friendship—or whatever this is. I just have to be careful how I tell him.

"Eason, you need to know something," I whisper. The gravity of my expression and tone shifts the mood in an instant.

He puts his finger to my lips for silence. "I have to tell you something too," he replies, equally cautious.

He pulls himself away from me and crosses the room. When he comes back, he's cradling a small wooden box. Instead of flipping open the lid on top, I watch as he slides a panel on the bottom, pulls out a wooden peg, and opens a hidden compartment. He removes a thin, jagged pin from the secret partition, and I recognize it as the key that was used to activate my intercuff the night it was put on, except this one is the color of tarnished bronze.

I open my mouth in shock, and he covers it with his hand before I can utter a word. He presses a finger to his own lips, cautioning silence.

Though I have a million questions, I keep my mouth shut as he effortlessly removes first his band, and then mine.

CHAPTER 16

"**N**ow they can't hear us," he says, no longer reserved.

This completely confirms my suspicion that we can be listened to anywhere, though I should have realized that the intercuffs are the perfect spy tool. This also means that all of my efforts to keep him from saying anything compromising over the past few days were unnecessary, and I feel silly thinking of all of my clumsy and hasty evasions and exits. All along, he was more aware of the danger than even I was.

I rub my wrist, and it feels so wonderful to be free of the shackle. "Where did you get that?"

"It was a gift. But that's not the point. We can't leave them off for long or it will be noticed."

Eason is full of surprises. I can't imagine how he came to be in possession of that device. I'm positive he's not supposed to have it. Right now, however, there are more important matters to discuss.

"Eason, Enforcers and the Council are watching you," I warn him. Now that I'm sure we can talk safely, I tell him the whole truth about how I actually crossed the Wall of Fire, and the trouble I'm in because of it. "They think you came back to the Burning for some nefarious reason, and they want me to find out what it is. I'm worried about you."

He laughs. "Seriously, they asked you to spy on me?" He doesn't seem upset or even worried. "And what have you told them?"

"I haven't had anything to tell. I've made sure of that. Every time I thought you might say something they would want to know, I changed the subject or made an excuse to leave, just in case they were listening."

"Of course, you were right. They were listening, no doubt," he mutters. "Well that explains all the abrupt departures. I thought I was doing something seriously wrong to upset or bore you."

I laugh and wrap my arms around him. "Quite the opposite," I assure him. "But Eason, I'm worried what they'll do to you. If they don't have whatever answers they want, the Council will send you to the Ash."

"Don't worry about me," he says, unconcerned. "There's nothing to worry about."

And then a thought occurs to me—too ludicrous for me to have ever considered before this moment. "Is that what you want, Eason? Do you want out of The City? Did you rank last on the Bronze Trial on purpose?" It's crazy to think that anyone would *want* to face the horrors of the Ash, but it's really the only conclusion that fits the facts.

"Yes," he says simply.

"Then why go through all of this? The maze was a

perfect way out. It would have been so easy for you to just not find the exit."

"True," he agrees. "But I wasn't expecting that. I wasn't ready to leave that night. My preparations are...delicate. Everything wasn't in place yet."

"Preparations? What are you talking about?" Sometimes Eason can be so cryptic, and I wonder if that's because he doesn't know how to just say something straight, or if it's a survival tactic he's learned through years of living in the Flame.

"The City is not what we've been told," Eason says, leading me to sit with him on the edge of the bed. "The Withers has been gone for ages, but the Council won't let go of the power they have here. The Safe Dome wasn't meant to stay up forever."

I can't believe what I'm hearing. Everyone knows that the world outside has been ravaged by the Withers. Roamers—the few who survived the disease—are all that are left, and they are savage. The hope of humanity is within the Safe Domes that shelter those who were lucky enough to reach them before the disease overtook them.

"You don't know anything about the outside. How could you? Eason, you can't leave—not on purpose. You'll die. What would be the point of that?"

"I won't die. I know how to bring the barrier field down and set everyone free from this prison, but it has to be from the outside."

I gasp and cover my mouth. Not only for his sake, but for the sake of everyone, I hope he's wrong. If he brings down the barrier field protecting The City, it will be overrun and pillaged in days. We'll be defenseless against the disease the Roamers carry, and unprepared for their desperate and wild attacks for food and other resources. Can I really stand by and let him do this? All my efforts to save Whyle will mean nothing if The City ceases to exist to protect him.

And then he hits me with another bombshell. "Emery, I want you to come with me."

"Wait, Eason. I can't leave The City," I protest. "Even if what you say is true—which I don't believe—I came here for a reason. I have to find a way to get that medicine to my brother. He doesn't have much time left."

"It won't be enough," he says.

"I have enough medicine for everyone who was sick. More, even."

"So you make him better now, but what about the next thing, and the next? This isn't random, Emery. It's not a normal illness. The Council is doing this on purpose."

"Why?" I demand.

He looks away, unable to answer.

"Nothing you're telling me makes sense, Eason," I insist, imploring him to see reason.

"Emery, I've waited for you for so long," he pleads. "I don't know if I can do this on my own."

"How could you have been waiting for me? I never planned to join the Burning," I counter, refusing to be manipulated.

"Okay, not you specifically—though I can't say how glad I was when I saw your name that night. Honestly, I was waiting for anyone from the Smoke. I need an ally, and only someone who has seen what we've seen would understand that The City isn't right and it can't last. It was never meant to be this way."

"The Smoke has problems," I hedge. "But we have food, we have a place to live, we're safe there. Our families are there. That's more than the Ash has to offer. Who knows if the other Safe Domes are even still functioning? For all we know, we're all that's left of healthy and civilized humankind. Whether or not this was the original plan, it's all we've got now, and that's all the more reason to protect it."

Eason is about to say more when heavy footsteps approach in the hallway. He leaps to his feet and replaces his intercuff. Three quick raps on the door announce someone's presence. Eason reaffixes my band, and the sharp, biting throb that signals its activation is just as intense this time as it was the first.

He walks to the door and opens it. Doctor Hollen and an Enforcer are there, looking as though they were about ready to override the lock. Surprised, the Enforcer looks down at the tablet he carries, and then back to Eason and me, wide-eyed.

"Are you all right?" Doctor Hollen asks, coming in and shining lights to check both of our eyes.

"Fine. Why?" Eason asks, sounding completely innocent. He's a good actor, I realize.

"Our mistake," the Enforcer apologizes, clearly confused. "A short lapse in signal led us to believe that you were in need of help. But it appears it was a malfunction. I'll have to check the receivers."

"I can assure you that we are both perfectly fine," Eason says. "Thanks for checking on us, though. It's nice to know that someone is looking out for us."

When they're gone, Eason turns to me. Our candor is over now that the intercuffs are active again, but a lot can be said with a glance, and he's begging me to believe him, to give up everything for him.

I'm shaking and terrified now for an entirely different reason than when I arrived in this room tonight. Terrance is right to be concerned about Eason. The only question is, now that I know, what am I going to do about it?

CHAPTER 17

In the morning, I don't want to go to breakfast and face Eason, so instead I walk in solitude around the yard outside while the other contestants eat. Despite a restless night and long internal debates, I'm still not entirely certain what I'm going to do about Eason.

If he wants to get himself thrown to the Ash, that's his problem. But could he really pose a threat to the entire Safe Dome? I can't rule out the possibility. He's done more than a few things that most people would say are impossible. For starters, he not only passed the Burning the first time through despite coming from the Smoke, but apparently did so with such grandeur that he received one of the most coveted assignments in the Flame. Then he chose to give it all up. And he has that secret key to the intercuffs.

What if he really has discovered some way to bring down the barrier field, and I say nothing and just let it happen? If knowing that Ty's death is my fault is eating me like a ravenous beast in my belly, how will I survive knowing that every person who dies at the hands of Roamers and the Withers is my fault, too?

I can't. That guilt will gnaw at me until I beg for

death.

I have to tell Terrance what I know.

With that decision, I feel better, but also worse. There are precious few people I've trusted in my life. I can count them on three fingers—Whyle, Mom, and Dad. For a moment, that circle expanded to encompass Eason—an ally in the abyss of the Burning. But I can see now how that was a mistake. It's always a mistake to get too close. The one thing you can always count on other people to do is to disappoint you. Not necessarily because they want to, but because they've got problems of their own. That's why I usually keep to myself. It's too easy to get swept up and find that other people's problems have spread like a virus and become yours, too.

I find myself near the greenhouse, and my stomach rumbles at the thought of the food inside. No one has said anything about the lemon and pepper that Eason gave me yesterday, so I decide there isn't much risk in popping in for just a minute to get something to replace the breakfast that I have chosen to forgo. But when I try the door, it's locked. A panel has been installed, and I scan my intercuff, but to no avail.

Disappointed, I turn away. Ashlyn's sitting against the wall taking slow, deep breaths, and I have to say she does not look good. I wonder how she managed to escape the maze, as frail as she seems. But that wasn't all about speed and physical ability. A fair bit of luck could go a long way there.

"Are you okay?" I ask her.

"I think it's the food this morning," she says weakly. "I hope it isn't a permanent change. Honestly, I don't know how you managed, Emery."

"What do you mean?" I ask, confused. I wasn't at breakfast, so I don't know what she's referring to.

"That gray mush they fed us. They said that's what the Smoke is served for every meal. It was awful."

"They served meal rations here?"

She nods.

I'm surprised—and disappointed if I'm not going to get real food anymore—but honestly, isn't that the best thing for the sustainability of The City? It makes sense.

"You get used to it," I assure her, but she doesn't look convinced.

Just then, a message appears on both of our intercuffs. *Report to the main hall for the Gold Trial.*

*   *   *

I'm the second to last to arrive in the trial room, followed only by Eason. I stay as far away from him as I can without acknowledging him, and the effort contracts and wrings at my heart.

We are all huddled in a small area at the entrance that has been walled off from the rest of the room. There's a palpable hum of energy in the air coming from the other contestants, and I wonder what they know that I don't about what lies beyond that wall.

Keya speaks to us from above. "Contestants, we have

finally reached the Gold Trial—the pinnacle of the Burning experience."

I don't like the sound of that.

She pauses as the final ring above us ignites in dramatic flair. Sparks rain down on us, tingling wherever they touch.

"In a moment, your path will be open. You will have one hour to reach safety," she explains. "This is your final opportunity to prove yourself to the Council. Be swift. Be brave. Be wise. Be pure."

As if that's a cue, the wall before us transforms to fog, and I realize that it must have been nothing more than a projection on a barrier field, much like the Wall of Fire itself. That's probably how they made the maze as well. I wonder how many things in The City aren't even real.

But as I consider this, I'm wasting time. Most of the other contestants have already crossed the fog, and I leap through after them. I will give everything I have to this trial. I'm so close to passing the Burning, I can taste it and smell it, and I want it like nothing I've ever wanted before.

Once I clear the sweet-tasting fog, I'm in a clearing at the edge of a forest with paths running in a dozen different directions. Most of the contestants have already scattered and passed out of sight. That makes me think that staying in the open isn't a wise plan. Didn't Keya say that reaching safety is the goal—which can only mean that this place is the opposite of safe.

I dive behind the nearest tree to observe, sheltered

behind its wide trunk. My foot hits something, and I nearly lose my balance. Looking down, I see what almost tripped me, and I can hardly believe my eyes. A blaster lies at my feet.

Timidly, I lift and examine it. I've never used one before, never even held one. The closest I've come is being shot with one just after being forced to enter the Burning. It looks real enough, though. It can't be that difficult to use. I find the trigger and practice holding it. I can throw a stone with pinpoint accuracy, so surely I can aim a blaster shot when the time comes—and I feel certain it will.

That's when the first whistle rings out, followed by a series of thuds like a shower of falling debris. I jump to my feet, press my back to the tree, and peek around to see what's happened.

Sinister-looking darts fly through the air, coming from high in a nearby tree. The attack appears to be directed at Eason, who is wandering around aimlessly in the open clearing—the only contestant in sight. If there was any doubt about what he told me last night—at least about his desire to go to the Ash—it is erased now. I know that he will never reach whatever safe haven is our goal, and the Council will have no choice but to expel him.

A dart catches him in the neck and sends him to the ground. There's no blood, but I'm guessing it must be poisoned because he stays down, moaning.

I'm so aggravated that he's brought on this attack right here. It's blocking my progress, and I'll never make it across without taking a dart or two myself. There must be another contestant in the tree firing at him. How many contestants have some kind of weapon now? I have a feeling this trial is going to make Vander's attack in the maze feel downright hospitable. But at least this time I have a weapon.

I sling the blaster strap over my shoulder and start to scale the tree in hopes of finding a vantage point that will allow me to spot the source of the attack. I climb as high as I can before the branches become too thin and threaten to give beneath my weight.

It's high enough that I can see not a person, but rather a black box set in a tree twenty feet away, from which the darts are being launched. It's not another contestant; it's a trap that's been set for us. I pull the blaster from my back and take aim. The first shot is too high, but the second connects, and the box falls lifeless to the ground.

I scurry back down the tree. The second my feet hit the ground, I'm running before another attack can be levied from somewhere else. I know that the smart move would be to make for the nearest path and take shelter in the forest, but Eason is writhing on the ground and I can't just leave him. I have to at least get him out of sight.

"Come on, Eason." I pull at his arm, and he mutters something incoherent and rolls away from me like I'm the threat here.

Annoyed, I pursue him. In addition to the dart in his neck, he's taken two more in his legs and one in his arm. I pull them all out, hoping that will help somehow, but I suspect that the full dose of poison has already been administered.

"Eason, we have to move! Let's go. I'm trying to help you," I say, keeping my voice low in case noise will trigger more attacks.

He looks up at me, and his eyes are unfocused. He smiles and starts to laugh. "You're really pretty, you know," he says, his words slurred. "Where are we?"

What did those darts drug him with? Whatever it was, there's no question that a hit from those will almost certainly wipe out any hope of passing this trial.

And then a plan begins to form that just might salvage everything.

"Eason, stand up!" I tug at his arm, and this time he doesn't fight me. I have him on his feet and we are walking, although I have to keep a tight hold on him or he starts to wander. But soon enough, we make it to the tree line.

Eason may have intended to thoroughly fail this trial, but he's in no condition to remember that now. If I can get us both to the end in time, I may just be able to prevent him from failing the Burning. That would save Eason without necessitating that I turn him in to Terrance and the Council while still protecting The City from whatever damage he's planning in his misguided attempt to save us.

I catch sight of Mieka and the spiky-haired guy running down a path to my left, so that's plenty of reason for me to veer right. I debate whether sticking to the path where we'll be expected is really the best strategy, but wandering aimlessly through the trees sounds even worse, so I keep us treading along the path at a slow jog, which is the most I can coax out of Eason.

The path forks every few yards, creating dozens, or maybe even hundreds, of possible routes. There's no way to guess which way is best, so I take alternating lefts and rights, which keeps us moving in a fairly straight line overall.

Traveling amid the trees with Eason at my side, I can't help feeling like I'm back in the maze. But this is sure to hold new challenges and unexpected tests, because this is the finale of the Burning.

After we travel about five minutes, beautiful birds swoop into view. I've seen so few birds in my life that I can't help stopping to admire their majestic flight and vibrant colors. But almost immediately, I know that this is a mistake. As soon as we are within reach, these birds, with wingspans as wide as my arms are long, begin to descend on us, diving at us like prey—first a red one, then orange, then green, then blue. The birds circle above us, taking turns diving at our heads, pecking and clawing.

I run for cover, but Eason just stares at them, unconcerned, as they tear into the flesh of his cheeks and shoulders, ripping through his shirt like it's paper. So I guess whatever was in that dart does something to deaden pain in addition to reason.

I take aim with the blaster, but the birds are too fast and only come into view when they're close, so I risk hitting Eason. Before I have time to consider, I sling the blaster back over my shoulder and run back for him, sustaining several large gashes across my arms as I ward off the birds and pull him to safety.

"Red, orange, green, blue, here they come to devour you," Eason begins chanting over and over.

I ignore him as I take aim again. This time, when the birds dive, I take them out easily. In almost perfect harmony, I bring down the birds as Eason calls out their colors.

"Red." Thud. *"Orange."* Thud. *"Green."* Thud. *"Blue."* Thud. *"Here they come to devour you."*

"Not anymore," I mutter to myself.

I take only a moment to assess our injuries and decide that none of them are so serious that we can't keep moving. Eason follows along easily as I get us back on the path, but he continues his little chant.

"Keep your voice down," I whisper.

I'm not sure if he's incapable of understanding me now or simply trying to spite me, but in response to my instructions for quiet, he ratchets up the volume and speed.

I'm glad that whatever is going to happen here is limited to an hour's time, because I'm not sure how long I can take the adrenaline coursing through my veins or deal with Eason's insanity.

"I wonder how much time we have left."

But, of course, Eason has no idea and ignores my question.

"Help!" The high-pitched cry rings out from somewhere nearby. I'm not sure which of the contestants it is.

"Come on," I say to Eason, pulling him in the direction of the screams.

The smart thing would be to run the opposite direction, but I wouldn't be here if someone hadn't stopped to help me in the maze. Surely I can spare a minute to lend a hand, or a blaster shot. I grasp my weapon and raise it, ready to fire at the first sign of danger.

The cries are growing louder, so I know we're close.

"Wait here," I instruct Eason. "Sit by this tree and I'll come back for you in a minute."

He does as I instruct, and I take another curve in the path. The trees clear away, and I stand at the opening of a small cave whose darkness seems to spill out and swallow the light nearby.

"Hello?" I call in a hushed voice.

"Get away from there!" It's the same voice that has been calling for help.

I turn to the sound and look up into a nearby tree, where Mieka's friend, Winter, is cowering. The legs of her pants are shredded, and blood covers the exposed skin.

"Winter, what is it?" I call back, unable to see the source of any danger.

"Run!" she yells.

And then I am overtaken from behind by a swarm of something that wriggles, and squeaks, and climbs, and gnaws.

"Rats!" I hiss, batting the vermin away.

It's no use; there are too many of them. As soon I kick or stomp at one, another takes its place. They climb up my legs and arms and back, scratching and biting all the way.

I drop to the ground and roll, which shakes off some but also picks up new ones.

I take Winter's lead and run for the trees, climbing. As the rats fall away, new ones fail to reach me. With the protection of height, I begin blasting at the horde. Normally rats don't scare me, but I've never faced more than one or two at a time.

They're coming from the cave, and every moment more emerge in a seemingly endless throng.

"Where did you get that?" Winter calls to me in awe, gazing longingly at the blaster.

"Found it near the entrance," I reply without pausing my attack.

"All I found was this," she complains, holding up a long, gleaming knife.

I get off another shot, but then freeze and take a closer look. I didn't think blasters could cause fire, but something on the ground is burning, consuming the rats—which are too focused on their attack to run for shelter.

Then another burning something is lobbed into the fray, and I know it's not the blaster that caused it.

"Get out of here, you pests!"

I cringe at the sound of Eason's voice. He's stomping through the underbrush and carrying a torch that he has apparently made himself in the time since I separated from him. He lights a small stick from it and throws it deep in the cave.

His strategy is working; the rats are dying. Smoke wafts back inside the cave, and soon, new rats cease to emerge. The problem is that he lacks the good sense to keep his distance, and he stumbles right into the mass of writhing, flaming rats. If I leave him, he'll be consumed by both predators and fire.

Can people actually die during the Burning?

If the Council is willing to send us to the Ash, I can't see how letting us die here and now is so much different, or worse—it might actually be a kindness in comparison.

I can't risk it. I have to get to him.

I leap down from the tree and run hard and fast for Eason. He's down on the ground, and I have to drag him to safety. His clothes are starting to burn, and I roll him on the dirt path to stifle the flames.

There are only a few rats still alive to follow us, and I squash them with ease.

Eason isn't moving, and his breath is weak.

"Winter, help me," I call to her.

The way forward is cleared now, and Winter scampers down from the tree. But rather than lending aid, she dashes off down one of the nearby paths and disappears.

"Eason, wake up," I plead, shaking him, but he doesn't respond. "Eason!" I yell into his face. "You have to wake up. We have to keep going." I tap at his cheeks and raise his head, trying to rouse him, but to no avail.

A menacing rustling comes from the trees nearby, and I know that the next attack is heading our way. I want to climb out of reach of whatever is coming, but I can't do that with Eason in tow.

Instead, I head for the only shelter I can see. Kicking the last of the burning rat carcasses from my path, I drag Eason to the cave where we will hopefully find reprieve rather than horrors awaiting us inside.

Once Eason is safe inside, I race back to retrieve the torch that's lying at the mouth of the cave. With fire in hand, I return to survey our sanctuary. The cave is a long, dark tunnel. The rats that remain are dead from smoke inhalation, and there is no sign of new dangers, but outside, snarling tells me that whatever was coming for us has arrived.

CHAPTER 18

I grab Eason and, as quietly as possible, drag him farther into the recesses of the cave. If whatever stalks us outside comes in, we'll be trapped. I head toward the mouth of the cave and string a line from wall to wall of whatever debris I can find, which largely consists of rat carcasses. Then I use the torch to set it ablaze.

"Emery," Eason calls weakly, and my heart leaps. I race back to his side.

"Eason, you're alive!" I am so overcome with relief that I fall down at his side and kiss him.

"I thought you were mad at me," he says, confused. "But that kiss makes it seem like you're not mad at me, which I like a lot better." He tries to pull himself up, puckering for another kiss, and it's apparent that his time spent unconscious has done nothing to clear his thinking.

"Just rest for a minute," I tell him, pushing him back. He collapses easily against my touch. "I'm going to see if there's another way out of this cave."

I secure the blaster and start to walk, torch in hand, into the unknown depths of the cave. Only the next few steps are illuminated by the glow of the firelight. As I go, I'm relieved to find the cave deserted, but it doesn't take long before I reach a dead-end.

I'm about to turn back when a flash of color against the wall catches my eye. I approach and find that one corner is filled with flowers, separated by color into vases. There are seven in all—yellow, red, green, orange, pink, blue, and white. The petals of each color of flower form a distinct shape. Each variety also varies in number, from one yellow bud on the left to seven white daisies on the right. It's far too perfectly arranged and out of place to be random.

I pick up the vases one at a time, but there is nothing beneath them.

I consider returning to Eason. He is singing something again. When the fire barricade dies out, he's going to draw in whatever stalks us if it hasn't moved on by then.

I hesitate, though; I feel certain that this means something, and if I can just figure out what to do, it will take us closer to our goal. I turn away from the flowers and check the rest of the wall for anything out of the ordinary, but it's just all solid stone. I step backward, taking in the scene as a whole, and that's when I notice four circles on the ground, each the same size as the base of each vase.

Hurriedly, I race and grab the first vase—yellow—and place it in the first circle. Then I do the same with the red, green, and finally orange.

The moment the final vase is placed, the ground shakes. The vases tumble, but do not break. I've done something, but it doesn't feel good. I wonder how many wrong answers I'm allowed before the cave collapses in on our heads.

There has to be a logical solution, and putting the first four vases with flowers in numbers one through four clearly isn't it. I need to reconsider.

While I think, I run back to Eason and make sure he's okay. He's standing now, which is a good sign.

"Come on, Eason."

I bring him back with me to the flower wall, so I can keep an eye on him while I work on this puzzle.

The minute he sees the colored flowers, he begins belting out his chant from earlier.

"*Red, orange, green, blue, here they come to devour you. Red, orange, green, blue, here they come to devour you.*"

My first instinct is to hush him, but then I realize that he may actually be giving me the answer. The colors in his chant are the order in which the birds attacked us earlier. It's as good a guess as any—probably better than most.

Hastily, I rearrange the vases, placing the red in the first circle, then orange, then green. When I set the blue in the final circle, the cave reverberates with a loud *snap*. I brace myself to run if the cave starts collapsing, but that proves unnecessary. Instead, just the back wall that blocks our path disintegrates into dust, opening a path forward.

"Blazes!" Eason exclaims, and rushes through the opening before I can pull him back.

For all I know, destruction awaits whoever crosses that threshold—be it by poisoned gas, or serpents, or a knife through the heart, I can only imagine. But nothing happens, and so I follow him through.

We are outside the cave now. Light streams down from above, as do the peering eyes of Keya and a dozen others watching from above.

A new path stretches out to our right, but straight ahead is a door. There are words inscribed on it.

> *Speak its name and be admitted to the safety this door provides*
> *Or continue on your quest for another means to this end*
> *It burns, but is not seen*
> *The fuel of the futile*
> *The plague which springs to action and deadens reason*
> *Which seeks to destroy what is*
> *And once has reached its object, ceases to exist*

"Eason, is there anything that burns without creating fire or light?" I ask, but Eason is staring up into the air, and unlikely to be any real help anyway. I probably shouldn't waste time pretending otherwise. I'm on my own for this.

I read over it again, and realize that it has to be talking about something less tangible. It's not about chemistry and fire, but emotion that burns unseen within us.

I focus on the rest, refraining from venturing a guess

out loud in case we'll be punished for wrong answers, as we were in the cave.

The fuel of the futile

The plague which springs to action and deadens reason

So something that drives people to act—to pursue the impossible without regard for logic. Something terrible—a "plague."

Jealousy? Passion? Both are emotions so strong that they blind us to rationality completely.

Which seeks to destroy what is

And once has reached its object ceases to exist

A destructive force that is satiated by the attainment of its goal. That's not exactly jealousy or passion which can burn on indefinitely, which are never satisfied at all.

But then I have it. I'm so certain that I don't think twice or act with caution. I just yell out the word: "Desire."

I wait, but nothing happens. I shove against the door in case it has unlocked without giving a sign, but it holds fast. At least nothing bad seems to happen, so I venture my other guesses, just in case.

"Jealousy."

Nothing happens.

"Passion."

Nothing.

"Lust," I add in desperation.

But nothing.

"Ten minutes!" Keya's voice echoes through the trees.

I don't know the answer, and I can't waste any more of

our time here guessing. There's another way around. Maybe it's longer, but we have to try. There's only one path to take from here, and I'm so grateful that I am spared the necessity of choosing a direction. I grab Eason's arm and pull him along, racing down the only path presented to us.

I can feel our time slipping away, and have to fight to remain calm every time Eason stumbles over a log or root and falls to the ground. Again and again, I drag him to his feet.

The path turns and extends parallel to a high cliff. We're getting close—I know it.

Rain starts to fall on us, and everywhere it lands, it stings and burns, leaving red welts.

"Don't stop!" I command. Eyes blurry and body aching, I gather all of my strength and run harder, willing myself to pull us through this newest attack.

Thankfully, we escape the acid rain quickly, and it doesn't follow us. The pain is torturous, but I can deal with it. Eason, on the other hand, doesn't appear to notice it at all despite the angry red lumps covering his arms and face.

From another fork in the path, Jessamine and Vander appear up ahead of us. As if their presence is a cue, rocks start rolling from the cliff above, blocking our way.

Vander fires a blaster at the base of a tree, and it falls over, creating a wedge that holds the rocks at bay and the passage open. I have to admire his quick thinking and precision. He passes under the opening, and Jessamine is right on his heels.

"Come on, we have to make it before that log gives way," I tell Eason.

But as soon as I say it, Vander blasts the log to bits and the rocks cascade down. I come to a fast halt and pull Eason back before he can be crushed by an enormous boulder.

I curse Vander. Would it have been so hard for him to just leave it alone?

I grab for my blaster and begin firing at the rocks, but they are much denser than the tree, and it has little effect on them.

"Maybe we can climb over," I say, but when I look at Eason, he is sprawled out on the ground, and I realize for the first time how deep the gashes on his legs really are. He's lost a lot of blood. He's not climbing anywhere. And it's not like I can drag him up.

I try to climb up anyway to get a look at what's on the other side, but the rocks are too loose, and they roll beneath my feet. From ten feet up, I come tumbling down to the ground and land with a thud that knocks the wind out of me. Breathless and aching, I jump back to my feet and race to attack the pile of rocks. I have to move them—to clear our path.

I put my back to a medium-sized rock in a crucial spot to clearing the blockade, but with all my might I can't make it budge.

It's been at least three minutes since Keya's announcement, maybe four. I don't have much time.

There must be at least twenty rocks that need to be cleared in order for us to pass, especially with Eason in his condition, and many are bigger than the one I just tried and failed to dislodge. The chances of me opening this passage are probably less than zero, and yet, against all reason, I pick up the smallest rock and move it, and then the next.

And when all the rocks that I can move are cleared, I put my back against another and push with all my might, panting, muscles throbbing with exertion.

I cannot accept that my plight is in vain. If I fail now, then I'll never be able to get the medicine to Whyle and save his life. I won't be able to save Eason from himself. I must not fail the Burning. I must not accept things as they are in this moment. I will find a way to create a new reality. If I can do that, I will forever be satisfied. But the one thing I cannot do in this instant is give up the one thing I have left—the only thing that sustains me and drives me forward despite insurmountable odds and crushing obstacles.

With a gasp, I stop pushing. I know how to get us out of here, but there's not a second to spare.

I race back to Eason, who's drifting in and out of consciousness. With great difficulty, I coax him to his feet and wrap his arm around my shoulders, holding on to support him as much as possible. Slow and clumsy, we begin making our way back up the path. How much time do we have? It can't be much. I just pray it will be enough to return to the door.

Eason falls to the ground, and I half-help and half-drag him back up. He groans and tries to bat me away, but I refuse to leave him when we are so close.

"Three minutes!" Keya calls just as the door comes into view.

But then Eason collapses, and this time, I can't wake him enough to get a single ounce of cooperation. Rallying all of my remaining strength, I start to drag him. Sliding along the rough ground only tears Eason's wounds open wider and leaves a trail of blood on the path, but it doesn't matter. Nothing is more important than reaching that door. Fortunately, this will be over soon, and Doctor Hollen will heal him. I don't know how much longer he can last like this.

My back aches, my head throbs, but I keep one foot moving in front of the other until my legs have turned to mush and refuse to support me for one more second. I collapse to the dirt just as I reach our destination.

> *It burns, but is not seen*
> *The fuel of the futile*
> *The plague which springs to action and deadens reason*
> *Which seeks to destroy what is*
> *And once has reached its object, ceases to exist*

I scream the word that is my answer and my driving force.

"Hope!"

The door swings open. With my very last vestiges of strength, I crawl to Eason and wrap my arms around his torso, then drag him as I scoot my way through the door. His feet clear the threshold just as the entire landscape evaporates into thin air—and so does my awareness.

CHAPTER 19

I awake in the Medical Center without a clue as to how much time has passed. Eason is lying feet away on the bed to my right, but we aren't the only contestants who took a beating during the Gold Trial. Jasper is on the bed to my left, and Winter is sprawled on the next one over. A girl with shiny brunette hair who I can't name occupies the farthest spot.

Everyone but Eason is awake and sitting up.

Doctor Hollen comes in, checks them over, and dismisses them one by one. As they leave, there are no traces of injury visible on any of them.

Finally, he comes to me. "How are you feeling, Emery?" he asks, shining a light in my eyes.

I tense and relax my muscles and find, with equal parts surprise and confusion, that I feel perfectly fine. "Good, actually. Nothing hurts. How long have I been out?"

"Just about thirty minutes."

"Really?" I sit up and examine my body. My clothes are torn, especially the bottoms of my pant legs where the rats clawed and scratched and gnawed away at me, but there is no trace of a break anywhere on my skin. "How did you heal me so quickly?" I ask in amazement.

The doctor chuckles. "There wasn't much to heal other than a few scrapes and bruises, really. Most of what you experienced was just an illusion of sorts."

"What? No, I felt those little beasts biting me. And what about Eason? He was burned. Blood was pouring from his leg." I look at him, but he appears to be perfectly fine and sleeping soundly. "He lost so much blood that he passed out. And what about the dart? He was out of his blazing mind the whole time."

Doctor Hollen nods. "It's quite amazing—fascinating, really—how effectively your body responds to what your mind believes. It was the fog that you all passed through on entry that made you so susceptible to believe whatever was suggested," he explains with the satisfaction of someone observing the workings of something beautiful and elegant.

I suppose that to a doctor, the intricacies of how the mind exerts control over the body would be enthralling. To me, it's just annoying and disorienting, but at least I'm safe now.

"You are free to go back to your room," he says, and then walks away.

The moment he is out of the room, Eason stirs to life; I suspect he's been awake for a while, just biding his time patiently until he could have a moment alone with me.

"Emery," he whispers.

I rush to his side and lean over to hear him better.

"Why am I here?" he asks.

I brush several strands of his hair from his eyes and rest

my hand against his cheek. "You were hit by a poisoned dart—or several, actually—during the Gold Trial. I had a really rough time getting you to safety, but we made it."

I'm not sure if he's going to be upset at this news—the part about me getting him through the trial that he so thoroughly tried to fail—but he doesn't seem bothered. "You shouldn't have wasted your energy on me."

"I couldn't just leave you," I protest.

He pulls himself to a seated position and shrugs. "It won't matter anyway."

"Eason, we made it. We both made it through the door that led to safety. That's what Keya said we had to do. We passed—both of us."

"Do you really think the Council won't realize that it was entirely you, not me? It's not about getting to a certain destination—it's a test of how we respond under duress. I doubt I impressed the Council in that regard," he says with satisfaction.

I can't really argue the point. The former Burn Master would know the measure of success far better than I.

Irritated, I back away and flee from his presence. All of my effort achieved nothing. Eason is still a danger to The City, and I risked Whyle's life in a pointless endeavor.

Worst of all, this means that I still have little choice but to tell Terrance everything I know about Eason's plans. The thought of betraying him is about as painful to me as the thought of shoving shards of glass under my nails, but I can't see any other alternative.

Alone in my room, I resolve to never again allow

Eason Crandell to distract me and threaten my one true goal. Today is the fifth day since Whyle became ill. Liam said that the disease progresses over two weeks. I still have time, but not much. Finding a way to get the medicine to him is all that matters.

I rifle under the bed where I stored my old shoes that conceal the vials of Curosene. My grasp is met with nothing but air, and fear seizes at my throat. I drop to the floor gasping and peer into the shadows, but there is not so much as a speck of dust, let alone shoes and life-saving medication. I feel as though the world has been ripped from beneath me, and I am plummeting into an endless abyss.

Fighting for breath and combating the ensuing dizziness that overtakes me, I drag myself up to my feet and search the room. The recycle bin is empty. The closet conceals nothing but new, clean clothing. Petra hasn't disturbed my old clothes under the mattress, but she also hasn't added my shoes to the stash.

Frantic and desperate, I consider my options. Perhaps I could fabricate an injury and return to the Medical Center to get more Curosene. But there's no believable injury I could sustain here in my room, so it's bound to be met with skepticism. Before I do anything rash or risky, I have to find Petra. Maybe she knows where the shoes are, and I can still get them back. The most important thing is to stay calm and not to raise suspicion.

My heart and head are pounding. Even though I want nothing more than to race out and run through the hallways screaming Petra's name until I find her, I restrain myself. First, I walk to the sink and run cool water, splashing it on my face to calm myself until the flush of my cheeks is mostly gone. Only then do I allow myself to leave the room.

I try to walk calmly and appear casual, as though I'm just out for a stroll to stretch my legs and pass the time, but when no one is watching, my steps naturally migrate to a jog.

I have to search through three hallways, pausing at each door to listen, before my efforts are rewarded.

"Petra!" I exclaim just as she's exiting one of the staff member's rooms.

She jumps and then laughs. "Emery, you scared me."

I grab her by the shoulders and shake her. "Did you take my old shoes from under my bed?"

She goes rigid and stares back, eyes wide.

"Petra, did you take my shoes?" I repeat, releasing my hold on her.

It takes her a moment to recover from the shock. "You mean those filthy old shoes that were falling apart?"

"Yes, those ones."

"I took them with the trash this morning."

"Where are they now?" I ask, resisting the urge to shake her again.

Flustered, she begins to ramble. "Did you want them? I just thought you wanted the clothes. I couldn't imagine what use you could have for those old, nasty shoes. I'm sorry. I just thought—"

"It doesn't matter," I cut her off, trying to stay focused on what matters. "Just where are they now? In the recycling?" Things to be recycled will be loaded on a truck—much like the one that brought me across the wall—to be taken to the appropriate processing centers in the Smoke. I've seen the truck lumber through the gates to the Burning Center the last three nights, so I know that it won't come for a few more hours. I still have time to retrieve them.

She shakes her head. "There's not much of those shoes worth recycling. I sent them to be incinerated."

"When does that happen?" I demand.

She checks the time on her intercuff. "They aren't incredibly consistent about when it happens, but it could be any minute now."

"Where is the incinerator?"

"I don't understand what the problem is. The shoes you have now are so much nicer. I wouldn't worry about them."

"Where is the incinerator?" This time, there's no mistaking the unhinged quality to my voice.

Clearly terrified, she rattles off directions.

Without wasting time for so much as a "thank you," I take off running.

The incineration room is all the way on the far side of the building and one floor down, in the basement. When I reach the stretch of hallway that feeds into the dining hall, I encounter a dozen contestants and workers milling around. Even Keya is there, so I slow to what I hope is a casual saunter as I pass through the crowd.

I'm only halfway to the next corner when suddenly Jessamine grabs my arm and shoves me into a small room that appears to be a storage closet.

"Hi, Jessamine," I say, trying to keep my voice light and airy despite my panic and frustration. "I was just on my way to do something. Can we talk later?" I don't bother pointing out how weird it is that she just snatched me out of the hallway and dragged me into a small, dark room.

I turn to go, but she positions herself so that she's blocking the door, and I know there's no getting by her without creating a big scene, which I would really like to avoid. I'll just have to see what this is all about and try to resolve it quickly.

Her features contort in a menacing scowl, made more ominous by the deep shadows of this dark room. I can't help thinking that the worst side of Vander has rubbed off on her. "Why did you have to come here?" she demands, her face just inches from mine. "Do you understand what you've taken?"

For a moment I think she knows about the shoes and the Curosene, and I don't know what to say.

"You could have lived your whole life just fine in the Smoke. But no, you had to come here and steal one of our lives away from us," she goes on.

"What?" I stammer, perplexed at the turn this conversation has taken.

"We don't get a choice, Emery. We have to come to

the Burning. There are only so many assignments to go around. If you take a spot, then that means one of us is out!"

I've never thought of the situation like that, but it makes sense.

"I'm sorry. But Jessamine, you seem to have done fairly well. I'm sure you'll make it," I try to reassure her. She had one of the highest ranks on the Bronze Trial, after all.

She laughs, and the sound is ghostly and frightening. "You think this is about me. You know nothing. You can't even imagine what you've done. I hate you for coming here."

Her hand flies at my face. I would have caught it, or dodged it if the lighting were better, but in the dark I don't see it coming soon enough. Her hand hits me hard against my cheek and it stings, but not worse than so many things I've already endured today.

This conversation has momentarily distracted me from my real goal, but that slap was just what I needed to clear my head. I need to get out of here—now.

I rack my brain for anything I can say to appease her enough to get her out of my way, and I settle for the truth. "Jessamine, I'm sorry! I promise, I didn't mean to hurt anyone. I didn't even actually want to join the Burning, believe it or not. Honestly, I would go home this instant if I could. But right now, you aren't the only one without a choice."

Something in my words seems to mollify her. She

considers, and then her posture relaxes. "Do you really mean that?" she asks. "You would go home, if you could?"

"Yes," I say, sincere despite the fact that it's impossible.

"I'm sorry I hit you," she says, and opens the door.

That's all I need, and I take off running, no longer caring who's watching. I can't let anything else sidetrack me from getting to my destination. If those vials are tossed into the fire, it might as well be Whyle being thrown to the flames, because his life is equally forfeit in either case.

The basement is a dank place with only one large room. When I enter, it's deserted. It's easy to find what I'm looking for. On the far wall is a hatch labeled *incinerator*, and next to it sits a bin.

I leap to the bin. It's nearly empty because almost everything in The City is recycled, so it's easy to find my shoes and snatch them from danger.

I'm relieved that I made it, but then I hear footsteps on the stairs. There's nowhere to hide, and if anyone sees me carrying these shoes, there will be questions about why I would ever wish to save them. I do the first thing that pops into my head.

Quickly, I slip off the good shoes that Eason gave me and put on these instead.

Just as I finish, a woman reaches the bottom of the stairs. "What are you doing down here?" she demands. "Contestants aren't supposed to be in this part of the building."

"Oh, sorry. I'll go." I scoop up the shoes and move to step around her and escape to the stairs.

"Hold on." She puts out an arm to block me. "Why are you carrying shoes around with you? Are those yours?" She examines the shabby shoes I'm wearing and squints in disapproval. She's not going to be satisfied without some kind of explanation.

"Oh, it's just that my good shoes got put in the trash to be incinerated by mistake, so I came to get them. Obviously it was these ones that were supposed to go," I say, gesturing to my feet.

"Was it that maid, Petra, that screwed up?" the woman demands, and I realize I might be getting Petra into trouble.

"Oh, no," I stammer. "Not Petra. It was my fault, really." I'm not sure how to explain that, so I'm glad when she doesn't ask more questions, but I'm still worried that I've accidentally created problems for Petra. I'm going to have to try and make that up to her later.

"I was just about to do the incinerating for the day," the woman says. "Go ahead and take those old shoes off and I'll take care of them for you."

Blazes! Why didn't I see that coming?

She watches as I slowly—so slowly—bend down and start fumbling with the ties, trying to stall. Eventually, she gets tired of waiting and walks past me to get started with her task. As soon as her eyes are off of me, I rip off the shoes and pull the vials from their hidden compartments.

I hear her rustling in the bin behind me, but I move

fast and keep my back to her to block her view. I'm only able to squish four of the vials in the new shoes, which are a bit tighter than my old ones. I shove the other two vials down my shirt.

"Here you go," I call as I toss the shoes across the room to her.

"Oh, my!" she exclaims as she sees their dilapidated state. "How did you even walk in these things?"

I don't stick around for comments or conversation.

CHAPTER 20

When a knock sounds at my door an hour later, I expect it will by Terrance Enberg coming to collect on our deal. I'm ready for him. But before I can get to the door, a frayed, folded paper is slid underneath. I fling open the door to see who delivered it, but they've already fled.

I shut the door again before I pick up the delivery and examine it. The paper is old, crinkled, and faded. I unfold it and study the hand-drawn lines in confusion. It takes several minutes of staring at it before I realize that it has to be a map of The City. There are lines leading from building to building throughout the Flame in the center, and from several of those buildings across the Wall of Fire and into the Smoke. Each line starts and ends with a short annotation such as "notch in basement wall," or "center floor plank." My hand flies to my mouth, and I gasp as the meaning dawns on me.

The tunnels are real!

I pace for a few minutes, trying to make sense of the situation.

This could be some kind of trap, a test of sorts. But that doesn't make much sense. All the tests of the Burning are carefully crafted and controlled in the four trials.

The most logical explanation is that Jessamine gave this to me. Maybe her parents work in the tunnels, and she's hoping that, armed with this information, I'll make a run for it and leave my spot in the Burning open. After our recent conversation, that seems like the most likely explanation.

I'm tempted to do just that. I can smell the scent of my mother's hair as she hugs me, feel the rough comfort of my old blanket as I snuggle into my bed at home. For just a moment, it feels like it could be mine again, and I ache for the familiar reassurance of it all.

But it would be pointless. They would come for me soon enough. I couldn't hide forever, and there would be no possibility for me to work. I would live like Kenna, though worse, because Kenna isn't being hunted by Enforcers.

My life is here now—if I pass the Burning. But the fact of my victory is not something I can take for granted when it's still at the mercy of the Council's whims, no matter how well I've performed. This may be my last night in The City. And that means that if I have an opportunity to get to Whyle before the Refinement tomorrow, I must take it. Then I'll know that Whyle is safe from the gulf that threatens to swallow him, and then what happens to me at the Refinement doesn't really matter.

I inspect the map again. The tunnel entrance within the building is located through a cupboard in the basement. I know the incineration is done for the day, and the room didn't look like it was used for much else, so there is a really good chance it's deserted now.

I take out the vials I've stowed under the mattress and turn them over in my hands. I need a way to carry them that doesn't involve my shoes or underwear. After a few minutes of consideration, I pull the broken, jagged nail file that I used to hollow the heels of my old shoes from the back of the drawer. Then I go to the bed and pull back the blanket. Using the pointed end of the file, I rip a square of fabric from the smooth, white sheet. I've had so few fine things in my life that the feeling of destroying something so nice is actually sickening, but I do it anyway. Then I rip another, longer strip. Using the knots I learned during the time I was assigned to the crew that washes windows—where a good knot on your harness line is the difference between safety and a broken back—I turn the square into a pouch and use the long, thin strip to create a strap. Though it may not be beautifully crafted like the bags I've seen some of the other contestants occasionally carry, it should do the job.

But I still have a serious problem. I frown at my wrist. There's the intercuff to contend with. I wonder what Jessamine expects me to do about that. Maybe she doesn't care if I go home while wearing it and the Enforcers snatch me up within minutes and deliver me to the same fate as Ty. Maybe she even hopes I'll be dumb enough to do just that.

Fortunately, that's not my only option.

Quickly, I retrieve my old clothes from under the mattress. I wasn't thinking about these when I made the bag, but by folding them carefully, I'm able to squeeze them inside and keep them mostly contained. That's good, because if anyone stops me to examine the contents of the bag, what they'll see is old clothes—too filthy for them to want to inspect closely—not stolen vials. I put the strap of the bag over my head and across my torso to keep it secure. I just hope I can reach Eason before he goes to the dining hall for dinner.

Seconds later, I'm knocking on his door with trepidation, trying to decide exactly what I should say to him. Our last conversation didn't end on the best note. Plus, I'm still planning on turning him in to Terrance if he insists on pursuing his plan, so that also puts a serious strain on things between us. Still, I have nowhere else to turn.

When he opens the door, his face lights up in hope, which quickly shifts to hesitation as he takes in my expression and appearance—particularly the fraying, lumpy, makeshift bag I carry.

He starts to ask something, but it's my turn to hush him. I push past him into the room and wait for him to close the door. When I gesture to our intercuffs, it doesn't take him long to understand what I'm asking. Within moments, they're both lying lifeless on the bed.

He reaches for me, and despite my better judgment, I don't pull away. His palm against my cheek feels like how I imagine sunshine. I desperately wish he hadn't said those things to me last night. In mere moments, the dreams I had carefully started to weave of a life with Eason evaporated into nothingness. No, worse than nothingness, because the void they once occupied will always be a deep, painful somethingness.

"Emery, please come with me," he says again. "You can trust me."

I notice how often he talks about trust, but there's no way he can prove anything he's said until it's far too late if he's wrong. How can he—a kid from the Smoke—know anything about the Council and the outside world?

"Eason, I can't help you. This is insanity! Please don't do this."

He doesn't answer, and I know his course is set. It's too late to reverse, even if he wanted to. The trials that determine our fate are over. But even if he could, I know he wouldn't undo what he has done. His gaze is sad and longing, but his demeanor is sure—no hint of fear or uncertainty.

There is no changing the results of the trials now, but if I deny Terrance his demands, I can still ensure my own sentence to the Ash. That's what Eason is asking—for me to willingly choose him and the Ash.

"I can't go with you," I repeat.

"Will you keep my secret?" he asks.

I look away. How can I choose between Eason and the entire City? What he's proposing is so horrific, I can hardly even imagine the consequences.

When I don't answer, he drops his hand and leans

closer. "I trust you," he whispers next to my ear, and brushes his lips across my cheek in a gentle kiss that makes my heart collapse in on itself. "What did you come here for?" he finally asks.

Flustered and frustrated, I realize how much time I've already wasted. Quickly, I show Eason the map and explain my plan. "How long do I have before the Enforcers get suspicious about my intercuff?" I ask.

"Not long," he says. "Remember how quickly they came last night? Maybe another fifteen minutes, but probably less."

"Blazes! There's no way," I lament.

"There might be," he says, considering. "I could wear both of them."

"At the same time? Would that work?"

"I can't wear them at the same time. They only work on right wrists. I'll have to trade them off every ten minutes or so, just to be safe."

I think of the intense stab of pain that comes when the intercuff attaches and activates. It doesn't last long, but how many times will Eason have to endure it before I can return?

"You would do that for me?"

"I would do much more for you," he says, and I have to look away from the intensity of his stare.

When I exit his room, the hallway is empty. All the other contestants are at dinner, and I realize that hunger is something else that Eason is probably going to endure on my account tonight.

Within minutes, I'm standing in the empty basement room and staring at the place where the tunnel entrance should be, but there are no cupboards as the map suggests, just the wooden planks of the wall. Unwilling to be deterred, I feel along until I find a board that's uneven with the surrounding planks. I dig my nails into the groove between the boards, and with a groan, I manage to pry it loose.

A black void is concealed behind the plank, and I immediately know I've found the right place. At some point, the cupboard must have been removed and boarded over to hide the tunnel entrance. With renewed energy and anticipation, I pull away the two boards below it, which come away easily now that the first has been removed.

The tunnel is black, and I haven't got anything to light my way. The incinerator burns just feet away, and I consider trying to construct some sort of torch to take with me. Managing a torch while I crawl along will be difficult, though, and what if something in the tunnel turns out to be flammable? Quickly, I rule out anything involving fire.

I check the map again. Three tunnels branch off this main path. The one that I need is straight ahead. I can follow the tunnel blindly all the way to the Smoke merely by feel, being careful not to veer off the main line.

I decide to go ahead and change into my Smoke clothes now, so I can keep these ones clean. I pick up the bag again and prepare to let the earthy blackness engulf me. Then I realize that I can't close the passage behind me. If anyone comes down here while I'm gone, my escape will be discovered. There's nothing I can do about that now, though, so I accept it as a necessary risk and plunge ahead.

CHAPTER 21

The tunnel is low and narrow; I can only move through it on hands and knees. I've never thought of myself as claustrophobic, but the longer I crawl along in the dark, the more the space seems to contract around me. I start to feel like I'll never reach the end, that I've gone too far to return, and that I'll suffocate and die below The City in this tunnel tonight.

Since my eyes can't see anything in the pitch dark, my mind is free to envision whatever it likes, and I start to see Whyle, healthy and vibrant again, playing in the streets with the other kids. He's a strong, smart kid. I could find a way to tell him where my books are. If he studies them, he has a real chance of passing the Burning himself when he's older. It's not nearly as scary as everyone always makes it out to be. I imagine embracing him again and eating real food with him—though that might be a thing of the past now, even in the Flame. No matter. Whatever we do, I just want to see him again.

But that would leave my parents all alone. I'm not sure Whyle could do that to them. My parents have a tough shell, but they're fragile underneath. Whyle notices things like that about people. Instead of distancing himself from the things that can hurt, he burrows through into the mushy center and tries to buoy you up where you're weakest. He'll know that they need him, and that I can get along on my own. He'll choose to stay; I'm sure of it. And that means that tonight might very well be the last time I see any of my family—the only three people on the planet I've ever needed.

I have no idea how much time passes from the moment I enter the musty tunnel until I finally reach the end. I feel damp dirt in all directions, except where I just came from. Carefully, I stand in the darkness and bump my head on wood.

"Ouch," I complain, rubbing the back of my head.

I start to panic, fearing that I've come all this way only to find the other end completely impassable. I put my arms up and shove as hard as I can. Finally, the board dislodges. Gentle night light floods in, and I am free. With the aid of light, I find a rope hanging in one corner that I can use to pull myself up.

Cautiously, I emerge above ground. The scent of chalk dust laced with mold assaults me, and I know I'm in the school building, just as the map promised. I replace the floor board and take special note of its location—tenth from the wall—so I can find it later.

It's only been a few days since I was in this building listening to droning lectures on topics much less interesting than the things in my books, but it feels like a different lifetime. It's crazy to think of all those days I spent here without any clue that a tunnel to the Flame ran just below my feet.

The school building is empty, and has been for hours. School ends each day at lunchtime so all the students can attend to their afternoon work assignments. We're rotated often, just like the adults. My most recent assignment was helping the construction and repair crews, but in the past I've cared for the kids too young to be given work assignments, worked at all three recycling centers, served at a nutrition station, cleaned windows, and stocked shelves at the market.

No one stays in one position for too long. It helps keep things interesting. It also means that we've seen and worked with just about everyone in the Smoke at some point. We all know each other, but just a little.

Still, if I'm seen, I'm likely to be recognized. I peek out the warped window. Most people will be at one of the nutrition stations eating their dinner now, but a few people meander through the streets. It won't be curfew for another couple hours, and I need to return as quickly as possible. If Eason switches the intercuffs every ten minutes, he must have already done it at least twice. I cringe at the thought.

I race around to the back of the building, where fewer people pass by. I dig my fingers in the dirt and spread the grime on my face to obscure my appearance. My muscles are begging to run, but that will draw too much attention. I make my way out into the street and walk just a beat faster than the other pedestrians, knees trembling.

I turn and duck my head down as I pass an Enforcer.

My pulse pounds in my head, but he walks right past, paying me no more attention than the dirt streaking my face. Soon, I am at the Medical Center. I slink around to the back where no one is watching and consider what to do. I can't very well traipse inside and inject Whyle with Curosene in front of everyone. And I can't just leave the medicine for the doctors to find. It would raise some serious questions, and I don't trust that it would actually get to Whyle in the end.

I have enough medicine with me for everyone who was sick when I left. I just have to figure out how to ensure that it gets to them without anyone knowing it came from me.

There's a high window in the alleyway that overlooks the patient ward where I last saw Whyle. I pile up a couple crates and climb up to look in and assess the situation.

What I see is so shocking that I lose my balance and tumble to the stones below. My cheek is scratched and my elbow bleeding, but I ignore the sting and scramble back up for another look.

Every bed that's visible from this vantage point is occupied. I find Whyle; he looks awful, but he's still there, which means that he's still alive, and that's what matters. I wonder why only Dad sits with him. Unwillingly, I search the faces of the other patients, hoping against hope that I will not find Mom among them. But then my gaze alights on her worn and shrouded form huddled in the far corner, and I relax.

I feel the seconds and minutes ticking by and know that I can't just stay here, but I also can't go inside with so many people around. Maybe if I wait until the middle of the night. But I can't do that to Eason. I have to get back as soon as possible for both our sakes.

I observe the people inside for another minute before I know what to do. It's risky, but it's the best I've got. I wait until all but one of the doctors has moved on to the next room, and only a few assistants bustle around the patients.

At the right moment, I leap from my perch and toss three pebbles at the door. Then I wait with bated breath. But it doesn't take long, and the door opens. I see the shaggy brunette hair I was hoping for, and I exhale.

"Liam! It's me, Emery," I call as he steps out into the alleyway, looking around for the source of the noise. I'm so relieved to see him that I almost hug him—almost.

"Emery," he repeats in disbelief, squinting to focus on me. "They said you joined the Burning, even after you told me that you wouldn't."

I ignore his implied questions. "Liam, listen to me. I don't have much time. I have Curosene. I thought it would be enough for everyone, but so many more people are sick now. I only have six vials."

"How?"

"It's better if you don't know. Liam, you can't tell anyone about it, not the doctors, not anyone. And you can't say that you've seen me. Just please make sure that Whyle gets it. You can give the rest to whoever you choose, but please make sure that my brother gets it."

He watches in confusion as I dump out the contents of the ragged bag I carry and shove six small vials into his hands. He stares at them as though he's never seen such things before. Maybe it's just something he never expected to see again.

"Liam," I whisper, hoping to break him from his trance, "give it to them. I have to go now."

"But you don't understand," he says, his voice like a ghost. "This won't save them."

"I know it's not enough," I say. "I'm sorry. It's all I could get, and I didn't know that there were so many—"

"No," he cuts me off, more forceful now. "I told you that Curosene healed Mina's dad, but he's sick again."

"What?" I gasp in horror.

"It made him better for about two weeks, but he's just as bad as all the rest of them now."

All the hope and purpose that has driven me through these last few days—days that I never dreamed I could survive—is seeping away into a bleak void.

"How many are sick?" I ask, even though I don't really want to know the answer.

"Thirteen so far, but more every day. One died yesterday, two today."

"So it's spreading. Why haven't you quarantined these people?" I demand, surprised at the lack of common sense. Did the doctors learn nothing from the Withers outbreak that nearly wiped out humanity and drove us into the Safe Domes to begin with?

"Not spreading," he clarifies. "It's not contagious from person to person. That much was clear from the beginning."

"If you don't know what's causing it, how can you be certain it isn't contagious?"

"That's the worst part—we *do* know the cause now," Liam confesses, grave. "There is something in the food that affects only the people with certain genetic markers."

"The food," I repeat in disbelief. "Are you sure?"

"There's no doubt. It's the meal rations that are doing it. We informed the Council two days ago and requested an immediate alteration to the formula, but the Council hasn't acted or even responded."

Two days ago!

That means that the Council knew this *before* they introduced the same food to the Flame. This isn't an accident, and it isn't going to stop.

It's spreading—and the Council is the carrier.

"If the food was changed, would the people get better?" I ask.

"The ones who can still eat, probably. And more wouldn't keep getting sick, that's for sure. But once they're like them"—he gestures toward the unconscious patients on the beds inside—"nothing but Curosene will help, and only for a while."

"Treatment which the Council is also refusing to provide," I say.

"It's like they want these people to die." Liam whispers the unspeakable, and his face betrays his fear as he says it.

"What's different about these people that makes them a genetic target?" I ask, searching for meaning and clues to a solution.

"It's an obscure recessive gene. We have no idea what it does," he says, regretful. "All of the testing has been done...unofficially, so it's taking some time."

I wonder who figured this out, and how they managed it. Where could resources like that come from in the Smoke?

Liam grips my arm, his expression serious. "Emery, you have to swear you won't say anything to anyone about this."

"You aren't telling people that the food they're eating could kill them?" I ask. "Isn't that wrong?"

But even before he says it, I recognize the truth.

"What good would that do when there's nothing else to eat?" he asks in despair. "The people would panic, and things would get worse in every possible way."

I know he's right, and there's nothing I can do about it. But I came here to save Whyle from the brink of death, and I'm not leaving here without accomplishing that mission, no matter what the circumstances. All the rest of it doesn't matter until I know that Whyle is okay, if only for a short time.

"Liam, I won't say anything about this, I promise. There would be way too many questions that would get me in trouble if I did. But I risked everything for this medicine. Please give it to Whyle and buy him some more time," I beg, shoving the vials toward him. "You can do whatever you think is best with the other five vials. Just promise me he'll get it right away."

"I promise," he says, pocketing the medicine.

"And never tell anyone I was here."

"Not even your family?"

"Not even my family," I say, though it hurts to utter the words. If I can't tell them myself someday, then it's better—safer for all of us—if they don't know.

I watch as he returns inside, then I climb back onto my perch and spy through the window. It takes a few minutes for him to get an opportunity, but Liam makes good on his promise with a quick, almost imperceptible injection to Whyle's thigh.

I can't see any discernible change in his appearance. He doesn't wake or even stir. The only indication that something is changing is in the rhythmic rise and fall of his chest as his breathing slows to a normal rate, giving me hope that the rest of his symptoms will soon subside as well.

I've done all I can here. I indulge in one last glance at my parents; their faces are pained, as though they've taken about all they can from life. If all goes well, I'll see them before Whyle's illness can resurface or anyone else can be taken by it, and I'll make them all safe for good.

I hop down from the crate just as an Enforcer rounds the far corner to the alley.

"Hey, what are you doing there?" he bellows.

I have two choices—talk or run. Anything I say—especially my name—is going to end in disaster, so I bolt.

I can hear the *thud, thud, thud* of his footsteps behind me, and I know that he's pursuing, but not really keeping up. I enter the school and slam the door behind me.

In panic, my mind goes fuzzy. Which board was it?

I claw at the eighth board from the wall—no. Ninth—won't budge. Tenth—and it comes away easily. I slide into the tunnel and pull the board over the hole just as the creak of the opening door echoes through the building.

"I know you're in here!" the Enforcer calls out.

Dim lines of light seep through the edges of the floor board above me, telling me that it's not securely in place. But there's no way for me to tighten it from this side.

His footsteps come closer, and I don't dare move for fear of making noise and drawing his attention.

He pauses just a few steps away, and I wonder if he's spotted the uneven floorboard and is about to investigate, to pull it away and discover my treachery. But then he goes on walking again, and the slats of light disappear as his heavy boot seals the board into place. He stomps around for a few more minutes, then seems to give up and leaves the building. I wonder if he's abandoned the hunt or whether he'll be searching for me till curfew. I kind of hope the latter. It would serve him right.

I purse my lips tight together to keep from laughing out loud. As it turns out, I couldn't have asked for a better assistant in my escape. With the tunnel sealed and all traces of my visit to the Smoke gone, I begin the return trip. I have to get back to Eason as quickly as possible.

We have plans to make. Together, we're going to free The City from the murderous clutches of the Council.

CHAPTER 22

Gasping for air, I emerge into the basement of the Burning Center. It's not like there wasn't air in the tunnel, so I'm not sure why it feels like my lungs are full of nails. The wall boards and my clean clothes are just as I left them.

First, I secure the wall panels back in place. Then I strip down and change back into my Flame clothes. I use the old shirt to wipe off as much of the dirt from my face as I can, then I toss the old clothes and my makeshift bag into the incinerator, destroying all evidence of my escapade.

A few people meander through the halls as I race back to Eason, and I figure they're probably getting used to the strange Smoke girl who's frequently running through the halls, so I just keep going. Slowing down will only give them the opportunity to notice that my face and hands are filthy, and my wrist is bare—two very big problems.

Breathless, I bang on Eason's door, but when I do, it swings open on its own as though it had been left slightly ajar.

"Eason, it's me," I call as I enter, just loud enough for him to hear.

But the room is empty.

Panicked, I run to the bed where I last saw my intercuff, but it's not there. I don't know where Eason has gone, but I know he wouldn't have left if he had a choice. He left the door open for me, and the intercuff must be somewhere that he thought would be safe.

I go to the closet and pull out the wooden box where he hides his secrets. When I flip open the lid, I am relieved to find that my intercuff is there waiting for me. It takes a minute of fumbling, but I figure out how to slide open the hidden compartment and get the key.

Wincing, I know I've succeeded in reactivating my band when the sharp, punishing shock bites hard at my wrist. Unfortunately, I have no way of knowing how long the intercuff has been stowed in the box. How long has it been since Eason activated it, and will anyone be looking for me because of it?

I manage to return to my room unseen, but any relief I feel is quickly swept away. I'm not in my room thirty seconds when pounding starts at the door, and Keya is calling to me.

I can't let her see me like this, so I strip down as fast as I can and leap into the shower. The jets of water assault me with icy stabs, but I barely notice.

Now Keya is calling me from inside my room, apparently having let herself in. "Emery, is that you in the shower?"

I have no idea who else she thinks it could be, but I call back anyway. "Yes. Is that you, Keya? Sorry, I've been in here a while and I didn't hear you knock. I'm just so anxious about the Refinement, and the hot water helps to calm my nerves," I say as coarse shivers seize me.

"Of course you're nervous, my dear," she cries in tragic sympathy. "What girl from the Smoke wouldn't be? But I'll say that you've got a better chance than anyone else I've ever seen. Well, except... But never mind that."

I wonder if she was about to say Eason—at least, his first performance in the Burning.

"You've missed a lot," she informs me. "Dinner is completely over. Now I'm supposed to take you over to the Justice Building to speak with the Chief Enforcer. Hurry and get ready."

I turn off the water, which has thankfully warmed nicely, and towel off. While I'm dressing, Keya taps her foot impatiently. "As though I have nothing better to do than run errands and fetch people on the night before the Refinement," she mutters under her breath.

"I'm ready," I announce.

Even though she's in a hurry, Keya isn't about to lead me around with wet hair, and she shows me how to use a device that dries it in minutes. Then I follow her out of the room, and only then do I have a chance to realize that I have no idea what I'm going to tell Terrance, and my stomach starts turning in knots. I wish I could talk to Eason first. He would know how to handle this.

When we enter the Justice Building, Keya hands me off to the nearest Enforcer—a burly man who must be solidly twice my weight—and strides away in a rush. I have to admit, it's impressive how she manages to achieve grace and speed in those impractical shoes.

"Miss Kennish," Terrance's voice booms behind me, bringing my attention back to the unpleasant matter at hand.

I swallow hard and turn to face him. My palms are slick with sweat. I remind myself that I have nothing to be worried about. The worst they can do is send me to the Ash. No—the worst they can do now is to keep me. I cover my mouth to stifle the uncontrolled laugh that erupts. For once in my life, I have the upper hand.

"I trust that you have some good news for me. A smart girl like you wouldn't dare tell me otherwise," he says, his face stone. He walks toward the room where our initial conversation took place.

Tentatively, I follow. I'm really not looking forward to being alone with him, even if there's nothing he can do to me that isn't exactly what I want anyway. But there's really no choice with the hulking Enforcer right behind me. As directed, I take the same seat I occupied the last time I was here, and can hardly believe it was a mere four days ago. It feels like the entire planet has shifted on its axis since then, and nothing will ever be the same again. Though I can't say for sure about the state of the planet, the world for me will never be the same no matter how this goes.

Terrance clears the room with a single wave of his finger to dismiss the other Enforcer, and we are alone.

"So, I've noticed that you've spent a lot of time with

Eason. The two of you appear to get along quite nicely. I sincerely hope, for your sake, that you've discovered what it is that brought him back to the Burning."

"If I had, wouldn't you already know it?" I ask. "Don't you and the Council keep tabs on everyone through the intercuffs?"

He smiles and nods as though conceding a point to an adversary. "We do hear some things, but the system is not as precise and foolproof as we would like. There's plenty of interference, and much could be said and done without our knowledge. I assume Eason has figured this out by now."

I can't imagine what Terrance would do if he learned exactly what Eason has figured out regarding the intercuffs, and why his, in particular, seems to experience so much 'interference.'

"If he wanted to tell you something in private, I believe he could easily have found the opportunity, and I think he did do just that. So tell me, Emery, what is our dear friend Eason up to?" he asks pleasantly, as though we're old friends having a little chat.

I do a quick assessment of the situation and realize that I have four options at this point, but only one that ensures the outcome I want.

My first option is to tell the truth—divulge everything I know about Eason's plans to leave The City and bring down the barrier field. Until just a few hours ago, I had planned to do exactly that for what I believed to be the safety of The City and everyone living here. But given what I know now about the Council using the food to attack us, the Council is a far scarier and more certain threat than whatever may lie beyond the barrier, and this is the worst option of all.

I could weave a tale of some innocuous reason why Eason has returned to the Burning. I could say that he couldn't handle the pressures of being a Burn Master and is hoping to get a simpler assignment. That would make sense of his purposefully poor performance. Maybe Terrance would buy it. I could still be allowed to pass the Burning without betraying Eason. But what if the Council took that into consideration and actually gave him another assignment rather than expelling him to the Ash, where he can carry out his plan? Bringing down the barrier is the only way to truly save Whyle, and so many others.

My next option is to make him believe I've failed. That I don't know what Eason is planning. That I never fully gained his trust. But he might accept that I gave it my best effort, forgive my failure, and allow me to pass despite my failure. I can't risk that, either. I want out. I will do anything to protect my family. And I desperately want to be with Eason, wherever he goes. I do trust him, maybe more than anyone else I know.

So I must give Terrance and the Council absolutely no choice but to send me to the Ash—and Eason, too.

"Why would I help you?" I demand. "You aren't really trying to help me at all. How do I know you'll even keep your end of our deal?"

His pleasant demeanor dissolves in an instant. "We've been through this, Miss Kennish. You know exactly what's at stake and exactly what's in it for you. As far as any assurances go, I'm the best chance you've got at this point, so you're just going to have to trust me."

I give a derisive laugh that comes out more like a strangled snort, but makes my point. "I don't buy it. Eason's right about you all."

This piques his interest. "And what is he right about, precisely?"

I roll my eyes and look away. That's one step too far, I guess, because my intercuff turns yellow. I work to appear impassive. I was focused on the Ash and completely forgot about this tactic and what they'll do to me here and now if I don't fall in line.

"Come now, you don't want to choose the wrong side here," Terrance warns.

I continue refusing to meet his eyes. I cross my arms in defiance and remain silent.

Terrance looks like he might snap something in half, and that he might like that something to be my neck, but he doesn't move.

Several seconds pass before orange light replaces yellow, and a searing pain assaults me. Unlike the pain from the intercuff, which stayed localized in my wrist, this pain seems to tap into my entire nervous system and send the same shock wave across my entire body all at once. It lasts only a moment, but it's not something you can easily forget.

I can understand now why Petra was so bothered by it and so diligent in the following days about avoiding its recurrence. I can understand now why everyone in the Flame seems to respond so readily to the mere warning of this sensation's approach that the yellow glow signifies.

"Just tell me what Eason hopes to achieve and you can walk out of here right now," Terrance coaxes. "I won't let it hurt you anymore, and you can still have a place in the Flame."

"I hate this place," I proclaim. "If I can't go home to my family, I'd rather go to the Ash."

Suddenly, my vision goes black. Though I can't see it, I know that the light of my intercuff has shifted to a menacing red. Every muscle in my body contracts violently. I try to fight for air, but I can't manage a single breath. And if I can't breathe, then how can I scream? And if I can't scream, how can I possibly endure this agony?

The instant the viselike pain releases me from its clutches, my body goes limp and I topple from my chair. My head knocks hard against the tile floor and blood pours from my nose, but I don't even try to move.

The vibration of each step that Terrance takes toward me pounds in my head. He shoves me with the toe of his boot, and I roll onto my back. Then he leans down over my cowering form, close enough that I can smell something bitter on his breath when he says, "Don't be a fool. I know he's told you something important. This is your very last chance to talk." Despite his proximity, his voice sounds distant and dissonant as my head spins. "There's nothing to gain by this."

Whyle's face flashes in my head, and I cannot be confused by his pleas and lies. I will do this for Whyle—and for every other person who has survived the worst of the world just to become a pawn to the Council and be discarded just as easily.

Slowly my senses return, but my resolve is set.

"I have...nothing to say," I manage with difficulty, trying to make my voice strong. But it comes out hoarse and strangled, as though I have been shouting for hours.

"This is very stupid of you. You can't possibly imagine what's at stake here. Nothing else was more important than getting that information. Nothing. You failed me; you failed the Council; you failed The City." He bends down on one knee so that his face is just inches from mine, and I can feel the hot humidity of his breath on my skin. "You failed," he repeats in a drawn-out whisper.

Then he straightens and sighs. "It really is a pity. You actually did exceptionally well on every trial. You even passed the Bronze Trial on your own. I didn't change your score. I merely hoped to offer you more incentive and perspective, which clearly failed. You passed every trial, and even dragged Eason with you through the final one. A true altruist—pure as they come. If it weren't for your lack of judgment and cooperation on this, you could be confident of receiving an assignment tomorrow. I hope that haunts you as you suffer in the Ash."

And then the world morphs into blackness, and searing red heat, and blistering cold, and biting, and burning, and slicing, and crushing all at once.

A pain I can't escape even in unconsciousness.

*   *   *

Something soft and warm brushes against my cheek. The pain has finally left me. I open my eyes and am rewarded with the sight of Eason's face. We are in my room, and he sits on the bed next to me, stroking my face and waiting for me to return to him.

"There you are," he says with a smile, but he's cautious, probably not sure what to think of my refusal to tell Terrance what he wanted.

"Eason, where were you? When I got back you were gone."

"I'm sorry," he says. "A little more than an hour passed, and then an Enforcer showed up at my door. I was afraid they were onto our trick, but they were just there to collect me for Terrance. He wanted his own chance to interrogate me. Fortunately, I was wearing my own intercuff when they showed up. The whole time, I was storing the deactivated one in the box in case anything happened. Turns out I was right to be cautious."

"Terrance talked to you, too?" I say weakly, imagining Eason going through what I've just been through.

He nods, and the hollow look in his eyes tells me all I need to know. Terrance was no easier on Eason than he was on me. Experiencing that kind of pain leaves marks that may not be visible on the outside, but are easy to spot if you've ever endured it yourself.

"How long was I out?" I ask, the hoarseness in my voice not fully gone yet.

"I'm not sure. I think about an hour," he says. "You must have fallen or something, because the doctor fixed your broken nose. The fatigue will take longer to wear off."

I wonder how I got back to my room, and how Eason got in, but I don't ask. I'm sure that if he can remove intercuffs, he probably knows a thing or two about door locks, too. Besides, there are more pressing things to discuss.

With difficulty, I pull myself up to a seated position. Before I say anything that might be compromising, I check our wrists; both of our intercuffs are in place. The skin around Eason's is raw and red, which must be a consequence of continually switching between our bands to protect me while I was gone.

I take his arm and raise it to my lips, soothing the angry skin with a kiss.

I can tell he's not sure what to make of that, but he'll know soon enough.

I bring that arm around my neck, and draw myself closer to him. And then I kiss him, and it's only then, after all that this evening has put me through, that I can finally breathe.

He pulls away, searching my face for understanding.

I keep my declaration purposely simple and vague so that no spying ears can use my words to stop us. "You're right," I say. "I know it now. I'm with you."

Now it's his turn to look like someone who has finally found air after far too long without it. He kisses me again. No matter how they brand me a failure tomorrow at the Refinement, I know I've won everything that could ever matter.

CHAPTER 23

I't's nearly nine o'clock in the morning when I finally wake feeling gloriously well rested. I suppose Petra won't clean the room until after the Refinement, which isn't for another hour.

I wear my hair pulled back in a simple knot, like I would have back home. There's no one left to pretend for. A simple, green canvas bag has been provided for each contestant to pack his or her belongings in. Once I leave today, I won't be coming back. None of the contestants will. Succeed or fail, we will all leave the Burning Center directly after the Refinement is complete.

Technically, nothing belongs to me, since I came with nothing but the clothes I was wearing, and I incinerated those last night. Then I realize that's not entirely true. The shoes are undeniably mine. They were a gift, bought and paid for by Eason and given to me because he saw that I was in need and took it upon himself to look out for me.

I know I should be worried about what's ahead, but I just can't seem to feel anything but hopeful, because I do trust Eason. The riddle was wrong: hope doesn't burn or destroy, it shines and radiates and enlivens, and carries you on its wings to a better place. If Eason says it's okay, I believe him. As long as we're together, we'll find a way.

My bag will not be empty. When she delivered the bag, Keya told me that I can pack one change of clothes, my toothbrush, and a comb. That's it. It takes me all of a minute to fill it, and that long only because I'm in no rush. I slip the straps over my shoulders to wear it on my back.

I practically skip all the way to breakfast. I'm not the only contestant who decided that today was a good day to sleep in. But it only takes one glance around the room to determine that Eason and I may be the only contestants in a good mood this morning. Those whose appetites have not been destroyed by nerves are disgusted by the new food, and most trays remain untouched.

Eason's already seated, eating the gray mush and waiting for me. I cringe and want to tell him to stop, that the food is poison—at least for some people—but I can't say anything until we're out of The City.

I debate skipping breakfast myself. My brother is clearly a carrier of the genetic marker that the food targets, which means I could be as well. But finally I decide that, either way, one more meal can't do me much harm when I've been eating real Flame food for days to clear my system. Besides, I don't know how hard it'll be to find food in the Ash, so I should fill my belly now while I can. I accept my tray and sit with Eason. I am keenly aware of Terrance watching us from across the room, but there's nothing he can do to us now.

"How are you doing?" I ask, noting with relief that the redness on his wrist has faded.

His response is slow, as though he's pulling his mind from somewhere far away, back to the present. "I'm good. Everything is all set," he says, and I remember how he told me that there were things that needed to be ready, and that's why he couldn't allow himself to fail the maze trial, which would have been the easiest option by far. "How about you?" he asks, probably wondering if I'm having second thoughts or regrets about my decision.

"Great," I assure him.

"Are you packed?" he asks, and snatches up my bag from the ground beside me.

"Yeah, but it's not like I had a lot to pack. Keya said I could take a change of clothes, a toothbrush, and a comb. I guess even in the Ash, she finds it intolerable to think of my hair being less than impeccable. But I don't own anything else. Hey, what are you doing?"

For some reason, he's started rifling through my bag. It's not like there's anything to hide in there, but I still want him to stop. When I complain, he zips the bag shut. "Sorry, just making sure you're ready," he mutters, and slides it back to me.

Then he reaches into his own bag and places something on my tray. It's a small brown square, but not at all like the bread. This is dark, dense, and smooth, and I'm not sure what it is or what I'm supposed to do with it.

"It's called chocolate," he explains. "It's pretty rare, but I have a friend with connections."

"I'm not sure I want to try anything else you offer me," I say. I'm half-teasing, but my mouth puckers involuntarily at the mere memory of the pepper and lemon.

"Sorry about that," he says. "This is to make it up to you. It's really good. I promise."

I venture a small nibble, and the taste is heavenly. I set it down with a frown.

"What's wrong?" he asks, confused.

"I knew I shouldn't have eaten this," I complain.

"Why? Don't you like it?"

"Too much. I think you've ruined all other foods for me forever," I chide, and break into a smile.

"I'm so sorry," he says. "Well, I guess I'll just have to take this back. I wouldn't want to ruin your life that way."

He reaches for the chocolate, and I grab for his hand to stop him. I snatch up the treat with my other hand and bite into it, but I don't release my hold on him.

Though I'm careful not to let my expression betray my thoughts, I can't help wondering what kind of food we'll find in the Ash. Will it be hard to feed ourselves? Will there be plants growing, like the greenhouse here? Eason must have already considered this at length. I know he has a plan, and we'll be fine. I just have to rely on him.

Then Keya is at the microphone, calling our attention. "Congratulations, contestants! Today is the day you have all been waiting for. All of your hard work and best efforts are about to be rewarded, or... Well, never mind. But the important thing is that you have all done your best, and the Council is ready to issue judgment. In a moment we will all proceed to the auditorium, where your family and friends have gathered to witness this grand event."

Eason and I exchange sidelong glances. Neither of us will have family or friends in attendance, but no one considers that.

"I will lead the way," Keya announces. "Please follow me in an orderly manner. And remember, this is your very last chance to make an impression on the Council, so please do not embarrass yourselves."

I wonder what people have done in the past that makes her feel the need to offer this warning. I guess with the eyes of most of the Flame on them, and the pressures of the Burning still pressing, some people may react badly, especially if they know they have failed anyway.

Eason and I don't speak, but he takes my hand as we walk. That's all I need to soothe the jitters that have started to creep up.

We are all ushered to assigned seats set up on one side of a wide stage. I'm not sure how we're arranged, but I'm forced to let go of Eason since my seat is the second one, and his is the very last on the opposite end of the stage. To our left, a platform raised three steps up stands below the four burning trial rings that hover in the air.

I catch Jessamine looking at me, and if looks could kill, I'd fall flat on my face right then and there in front of hundreds of cheering onlookers. I know she was hoping to get rid of me when she delivered that map. While I'm still here, it did work, in a sense. Because of what I learned last night, I have willingly relinquished my place in the Flame, and that's all she cared about in the end, anyway. I can't tell her this, of course, but I know she'll feel better in a few moments when my fate is announced.

Jessamine had the good luck to be seated next to Vander, but they're either distracted by nerves or their relationship has cooled again, because they don't even acknowledge each other.

Keya stands at a microphone and addresses the audience. I don't bother listening to what she says. I'm too busy searching the audience. This is my first chance to see all of the murderous faces of the Council for myself. Surely they're here somewhere, but who could tell in this sea of faces?

"Gaven Lark!" Keya exclaims, and the freckle-faced boy seated to my left stands and walks. Legs shaking, he scales the steps to the top of a platform in the center of the stage.

I scan the audience. The auditorium is the largest room I've ever been in, and the seats of the audience are filled to capacity with more people standing along the walls. There must be at least three hundred people in all, and not a single one of them here for me. But there are a few people—five, to be exact—who I am interested to see.

"Where is the Council?" I whisper to Ashlyn, who's seated to my right.

She looks aghast that I would speak while we sit on the

stage. Perhaps this is exactly the kind of thing that Keya was warning us against.

Ashlyn purses her lips and gives an almost imperceptible shake of her head in response.

I guess that's fine, because I've missed the announcement of Gaven's results, but he's taken a seat on the other side of the stage, so that means that he has passed and received some kind of assignment.

"Emery Kennish!" Keya intones my name like a song.

Now I wish I had paid more attention to Gaven so I would know what to do, but it seems pretty simple. I pick up my bag, cross the stage, and mount the platform.

"Emery came from the Smoke. She made a heroic effort, better than any of us could have realistically hoped for, I dare say," Keya says, and I think she's trying to be complimentary. "Let's see how she fared. Have you proven your purity and worth to The City?" she says as though she's as interested as everyone else to discover the results, which is strange, because isn't she the one who announces them?

But then the four blazing rings above my head shift and line up in a vertical column above me like stacked halos. Even though I know it's not real fire, I can't help flinching as the rings descend around me, covering me in tingling flames just like the Wall of Fire is made of. When the rings rise and the pillar of fire recedes, I am left with a burnt and ashen appearance covering me from head to toe. This must be the signal that says that I have failed and am destined for the Ash.

I sigh in relief and steal one last glance at Eason. He offers me a brief, reassuring smile as the ashen effect fades.

An Enforcer is there to lead me from the stage. The room erupts in cheers, and even though I don't know any of these people, it still hurts a little that they so universally wish me gone. I'm glad I won't have to stay here with them after all. At least Keya has the kindness to appear genuinely upset, which makes me like her better.

Rather than leading me to the seat next to Gaven, the Enforcer escorts me off the stage to a small cagelike area surrounded by bars, from which I can witness the rest of the Refinement.

Ashlyn is already in place on the platform, and she looks ill again as she awaits the determination of her fate. When the rings and the pillar of fire leave her, she shimmers like a million speckles of gold. She is assigned to be a caregiver of the preschool children and claims the seat next to Gaven.

Next is Jasper, the boy who was with Vander in the maze. While he didn't actually attack me, he did nothing to defend me, either. I almost think that being sent to the Ash would serve him right, but then I remember that this would mean he would be with me. I sigh in relief when he begins to radiate glimmering gold. As long as he's not with me, I don't really care what his assignment is, but even I can't help being a little surprised when Keya announces the Council's decision.

"Burn Master."

He looks plenty surprised and delighted himself.

It's of no importance to me, though, who the next Burn Master will be. In fact, if Eason can really do what he's claimed, there may never be another round of the Burning—ever.

Next is Mieka. I'm betting she gets assigned to be an Enforcer, so she can spend her days intimidating and spitting at the people of the Smoke. But when the ashen cloak pronounces her fate in the Ash, I go rigid.

I watch, stunned, as the Enforcers bring her to occupy the small, enclosed space with me, and I feel anything but safe. My only consolation is that soon Eason will be here, and he's bigger and stronger than Mieka.

It turns out that I have nothing to worry about at the moment. She focuses all her attention on rattling the bars and yelling until an Enforcer has little choice but to neutralize her with a stun blast in order for the Refinement to proceed. The crowd seems to really be enjoying the lively show—a girl from the Smoke gone Ash, a new Burn Master, and now a stunning. What could make this Refinement more epic and memorable than that?

When it's Jessamine's turn, she actually looks happy, so I guess my results managed to cheer her up. She receives the assignment of nutrition worker. Her face is unreadable at that, and I'm guessing that the assignment would have been more appealing before the food change that took place just yesterday. Still, like Petra said, any assignment is good.

Vander follows her, and he looks so pale that I wonder

if he's going to collapse right on the stage. Maybe he caught something from Ashlyn the other day during the medical exam of the Silver Trial. I've never seen him look anything but confident—unless you differentiate arrogant—but perhaps that was all a façade. Vander scored at least in the middle of the pack on all the trials, so his position seems pretty safe.

That is perhaps why the crowd can only sit in silent shock when the fire leaves and the ashen pallor remains. Vander stays frozen on his perch at the top of the platform as though he's turned to stone, not ash, and the Enforcer has to pull him down and drag him away.

Jessamine is the only one who doesn't remain silent. Her sobs reverberate in a ghostly echo throughout the room. Maybe she knew something I didn't, and it was for Vander's sake that she fought so hard for every available assignment in The City, but her efforts were in vain.

A part of me can't help wondering if these specific people have been failed just to torment me, but I doubt I could merit that much consideration. Besides, in his current state, Vander doesn't pose a threat to anyone. He doesn't even look at me, just collapses to the ground and stares off in a catatonic stupor. I'm not sure what to do. Should I say something? But I don't know if I'm dealing with nice Vander or mean Vander. I wonder if the instability of his personality has something to do with his failure. Isn't the Council looking for reliability as much as anything?

And that reminds me—the Council.

"Vander," I whisper.

He turns to me, eyes unfocused.

"Vander, where is the Council? I want to see what they look like."

He gives a snide huff and rolls his eyes. "They don't come to this in person. They're too busy ruining everyone's lives."

"What?" I say in disbelief. How can the Council pass life-altering judgment on all of us and not even be bothered to show up and look us in the face?

Cowards.

Winter and the other remaining contestants receive assignments, but I miss what they are because I just don't care. Thirteen have gone, and only three so far have been sentenced to the Ash. With Ty missing—my stomach tightens at the thought of him—Eason is the fourteenth and final contestant to be judged.

Eason is called forward, and I watch with bated breath, anticipating the moment when he'll be at my side again and everything will finally feel right.

Keya can do nothing to keep the audience quiet as Eason—the talk of the Flame, I'm sure—mounts the platform and awaits judgment. He's probably the reason the audience is so packed that all the chairs are filled and people stand, lining the walls. It isn't until several hundred yellow flashes illuminate the room that Keya can finally be heard.

She keeps her remarks short. "Eason Crandell has returned to the Burning, giving up one of the most prestigious assignments imaginable. Now we will see how he can best serve The City."

For a final time, the flaming rings shift and descend, bringing down a column of fire around him.

I'm anxious for this to be over. As the rings ascend, I have to blink several times to make sure I'm not seeing things. But the shimmer coming off his hair, his face, his clothes—everywhere—is no trick of my eyes.

Eason has *passed* the Refinement.

"Eason Crandell," Keya's voice booms in satisfaction, "the Council, in its wisdom, has assigned you…"

My mind reels. This is a mistake. He did everything possible to ensure he would fail and be able to escape The City.

"…to the Council."

CHAPTER 24

The room erupts into cheers, and it's my turn to collapse and stare off in disbelief.

How can this be?

I grab the bars and pull myself back up to look at Eason, but Terrance Enberg is already escorting him off the stage.

"Eason!" I yell. "Eason!" But my voice is drowned in the roar of the crowd.

He's turned away, and I want him to look at me. I need to see his face and read his eyes. I need to understand. It's not until he's almost out of sight completely that he turns for a brief moment and finds me. His eyes are sad and pleading, but I can't make sense of his expression.

"Eason!" I call again, but he's gone.

"Figures," Vander huffs.

"What do you mean?" I demand, dropping to the floor next to him so I can hear over the din of the crowd.

But he doesn't have a chance to answer, because he's being pulled to his feet by a scruffy-faced Enforcer. An intimidating woman who's built like a brick building restrains Mieka, who has woken up and is more enraged than ever. At least her kicks and punches aren't aimed my way. The third Enforcer, a man who just looks bored, takes hold of my arm and I realize that this is the same Enforcer who apprehended me the night I crossed the Wall of Fire and delivered me to the Burning. I barely have a chance to grab for my bag before he's leading me out of the cage.

The six of us travel down a dark, narrow hallway that I think must be used only for this purpose; it's the one place in the Flame where I've ever seen dust or cobwebs. When we reach the end of the passage, a door is opened to the outside. I have to squint against the bright sky light as I emerge from the dimness inside, and I realize with an overwhelming and possibly unreasonable delight that today I will see the real sky—not this empty projection— and feel actual sunshine on my skin. I'll watch the clouds and dance under a rainbow.

But my giddiness is fleeting because, whatever I see or do today, I'll do it alone. The smothering blanket of hopelessness descends and threatens to strangle me.

But this isn't just about me—not by a long shot.

More important than what awaits me is what will happen to my family. Liam said that the sickness reemerges several weeks after receiving the Curosene. I have to free them before that, but I have no idea how Eason intended to accomplish that feat.

There is a car waiting for us. It's the first time I've ever ridden in a car, if I don't count my stolen ride on the courier truck that brought me into the Flame just five days ago. Just five days and everything has changed, and changed again, like a pendulum swinging, and now it's coming down for a final descent that will seal the nail in my coffin.

Mieka is yelling obscenities and stretching her limbs out to make it impossible for all three Enforcers together to stuff her inside the vehicle. She should have seen it coming, because I'm not one bit surprised when the stout female Enforcer pulls out her blaster and stuns Mieka a second time. Unconscious, they have no trouble heaping her in the seat next to me.

I watch the sparkling buildings of the Flame pass by and think that this was almost my home. After a lifetime of fearing the Burning, it turns out that I could have passed after all. I wonder how many others from the Smoke could do every bit as well as I did, and maybe better, if they weren't so terrified to try. They would need a better education, though. The books I studied in secret were essential. But if Eason could be assigned to the Council despite achieving the lowest ranks, then maybe the scores don't mean that much, anyway.

If things were different, I might be planning my new life here. For the briefest time, I did think that was the path my life might actually take. But I don't know that I ever could have truly belonged.

And maybe that's why the Refinement perplexes me so much—I don't understand this place and these people because I didn't grow up here and was never really meant to be here. After all, Eason's assignment didn't surprise everyone.

"Vander," I say, breaking the silence. He's staring out the window too, probably bidding goodbye to all he's ever known.

"Huh?" He doesn't look at me.

"Vander, what did you mean back there when you said 'it figures' about Eason?"

He shrugs. "It can't really be a surprise that he would end up on the Council."

"But why?" I demand, unable to venture a guess as to what he means. All the evidence points to a very different outcome. "He's from the Smoke. He had terrible rankings on most of the trials. It makes no sense at all."

"Maybe not if it were you or me, but with his dad being who he is…" Vander lets the words hang, as though the rest is self-explanatory.

"What do you mean? Eason grew up in the Smoke with just his mom. His dad has been dead since he was a baby. He can't have been anyone important."

Vander laughs. "Wow, you don't know anything about him, do you? I have no idea why he grew up in the Smoke, but his daddy is Breton Crandell, a member of the Council and very much alive."

What?

No.

He's the son of a councilman!

I have to mull that over and try to reconcile it with everything I know—which I'm starting to realize isn't much at all.

Then a few disparate comments click and finally make some sense. That's why he was so sure that his dad wished for him to join the Burning the first time around. That also has to be where he got the intercuff key, which he said was a 'gift.'

If Eason really did rejoin the Burning in order to make a bid for the Council with his father's approval, then everything that Terrance had me doing was meaningless.

Unless Eason wasn't really my test at all.

Maybe I was his test—and he passed, and I failed.

The icy sting of betrayal stabs at my gut in an attempt to eviscerate me.

I was right to not trust Eason, but he fooled me so completely. He must have had help all along the way. He knew exactly where to find me in the maze, exactly what to say to make me trust him. I wonder if it was actually him who gave me that map to the tunnels and not Jessamine.

I remember the guilt and pain I felt thinking of all the times he switched off our intercuffs and endured the punishing sting of activation to keep me safe, but that wasn't necessary at all, was it? He probably spent the time I was gone laughing at my stupidity. His story about being interrogated by Terrance just before me was certainly a lie as well.

He even knew my shoe size. I scowl at my feet now and move to rip his treacherous gift off. But the practical part of me that wants to survive the Ash wins out, and I manage restraint.

All the pieces start to fit nicely in one sickening picture. All except why anyone would go to all this trouble over me. And also why Eason grew up in the Smoke with only his mother—that still doesn't make any sense at all.

My face burns with anger and hurt and embarrassment, and I'm so glad no one is looking at me. I wipe away hot tears with the back of my hand.

Eason really is a good actor. I truly believed he cared about me, fell for his words when he said he needed me, melted into his embrace when he held me and kissed me as though we belonged together.

But that was all foolishness, and I deserve exactly what I'm getting for letting my heart cloud my judgment and prevent me from seeing what was so clearly right in front of me. I suppose the riddle had it right after all: hope is a plague that drives us to disregard what is right in front of our eyes in a futile attempt to change reality.

Hope burns and leaves scars.

We cross the Wall of Fire, and the familiar gloom of the Smoke envelops us. There's nothing I wouldn't give to undo the last few days and go back to the simple life I had before, when everything was a predictable struggle. But even knowing everything I know now, I would do it again, even if all it bought was a few more weeks of life for Whyle.

I'll just have to pray that Liam was wrong about the sickness.

We're in an area of the Smoke I've never seen before.

Back beyond the high towers of the water plant where I didn't know anything existed, we reach a building that looks deserted, but as the car approaches, the wide double doors swing open and the car drives right inside. Once we're clear of the doorway, the entrance closes once again, and I can't help thinking of a tomb being sealed shut.

I know we're at the edge of The City, so this must be our final destination—the gateway to the Ash, the point of no return.

I've been so distracted by the insane and shocking turn of events this morning that the reality of what's about to happen hasn't even set in. I know it hasn't because I'm still breathing normally, my hands aren't shaking, and I'm still thinking about my life in terms of decades rather than days. But when the car comes to a halt and an Enforcer pulls me from the lit interior to face the gloom of a dark tunnel, all of that starts to shift.

I look to Vander, but he's just as despondent as ever.

Mieka has just started to recover, which is lucky for her, but not so much for us.

Packs on our backs, the Enforcers march us down the dim passage until we reach a solid brick wall. All three of the Enforcers hold up their intercuffs to a sensor on the wall and force the three of us to do the same. Then a large section of the wall before us transforms to a translucent haze. It isn't like the fog we passed through to enter the Gold Trial, thank goodness, but it still prevents us from getting a clear look at what's beyond the barrier field.

My Enforcer—the one who started and ended my

time in the Burning—taps three bricks in a careful pattern and then watches with detachment as another brick slides aside, and a small black box comes out. The Enforcer takes it, and from it retrieves a jagged, silver pin that I'm now all too familiar with. He uses it to take off my intercuff, which is the one good thing that's happened to me today. Mieka allows him to do the same, which is the first thing she hasn't fought, so maybe she's starting to accept the situation. But when he tries to do the same to Vander, something inside him snaps.

"No! No! You can't take it," he yells, thrashing. "Don't deactivate it!" He cradles his right arm against his chest, trying to protect it.

I wonder what good he thinks the intercuff will do him in the Ash.

It takes all three of the Enforcers to subdue Vander. It seems like they're about to use a blaster on him, and I plead for him to stop fighting. What good will it do any of us to fight now? Hasn't Mieka already demonstrated the outcome of that? One stun shot will be all it takes to knock us out long enough for them to dump us, unconscious, into the open and hostile Ash. I don't know about Vander, but I want to be prepared to run if there are any Roamers around when we get there.

Besides, if any one of these Enforcers doesn't bother with a stun shot and goes straight for the kill shot, who would ever know or care? I might be begging for death soon enough, but before that, I really do want to see the sky with my own eyes.

But then my Enforcer has Vander's deactivated intercuff in his hand, and Vander gives up fighting.

"All right you three, time to go," Scruffy-Face says with a sneer. He's the only one who actually seems to be enjoying this situation.

I'm both surprised and a little relieved when Mieka leaps forward and disappears through the opening, leaving Vander and me behind.

I'm not sure I can face the unknown alone. I was counting on having Eason by my side at this moment, but that's not happening for obvious reasons. Vander is all I have right now. I'm not sure what good he'll be, but I reach over and take his hand anyway.

"Come on," I say. "It's our only choice."

He inhales a deep breath, and we take the few steps that bring us to the gateway.

What has the world become in the decades that The City has sheltered us—one of the few surviving groups of healthy, civilized humanity? Will Roamers be waiting for us, hoping we've brought something that can help them survive and lying in wait to ambush?

If anyone is waiting, they're going to be sadly disappointed with what our packs have to offer. It would be nice if someone would have packed us a lunch or given us a knife for protection and to help us get food. All I can do to protect myself is to throw a shoe at someone's head, or try to strangle them with my spare pants—so really, I just need to be ready to run.

"On three," I whisper. "One…two…three."

I have to tug Vander a little to get him to come, and I think Scruffy-Face helps him along with a little shove. The haze envelops us in a tingling embrace, and then relinquishes us to the unknown beyond.

The Story Continues…

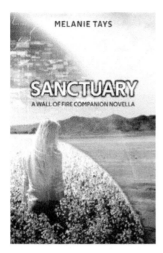

SANCTUARY (FREE ebook)
A Wall of Fire Companion Novella

Tech-savvy and independent, Mara has never felt like she belongs in the perfect utopia of Sanctuary. When the opportunity arises to leave and explore the treacherous, unknown world beyond, she volunteers. But in training she discovers that success could be the ultimate failure.

Download the FREE ebook
MelanieTays.com/book/sanctuary

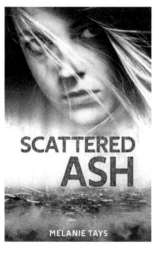

SCATTERED ASH
Wall of Fire Series Book 2

After being exiled from the protection of The City, Emery grapples with her new existence in the Ash and the aftermath of a crushing betrayal. Soon Emery discovers that the Ash isn't what anyone thought, and the truth is more horrifying than anyone could have imagined.

MelanieTays.com/book/scattered-ash

ABOUT THE AUTHOR

Melanie Tays is an author of young adult, speculative fiction. She loves stories with twists you don't see coming, intriguing questions, and satisfying answers. She spends her days imagining how the world could be different and then takes readers along for a surprising and exciting ride.

Melanie lives in Arizona with her husband, Chris, and two brilliant daughters who keep life interesting.

Learn more about her and her latest books at MelanieTays.com.

Printed in Great Britain
by Amazon

32127515R00142